To T...

CHINA STRONG

A Backpacker's Adventure

By Joyce Phillips

Joyce Phillips

Copyright © 2018 by Joyce Phillips

Phillips, Joyce
China Strong / by Joyce Phillips
Summary: A woman finds adventure and romance while backpacking through China.

ISBN: 978-1979010559

Published in the United States of America

Dedication

To Sasha, A Siamese cat who gave 14 years of unconditional love.

And to Sally, a childhood imaginary friend, who became an adult muse.

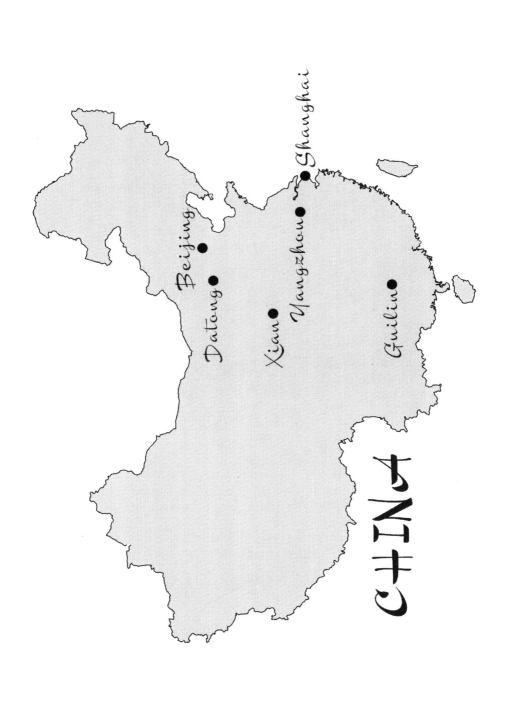

Beijing
Datong
Xian
Yangzhou
Shanghai
Guilin

CHINA

CAPE COD

SALLY

Sally Raymond was surrounded by bright, cheerful flowers in her Cape Cod garden. Purple delphiniums, white daisies and pink roses added their fragrances to the salt air blowing in from the Atlantic Ocean. She held today's bouquet and started toward her kitchen. Canada geese flew overhead and honked a greeting. "Good Morning!" she called and opened her kitchen door with a smile.

After filling a vase with water, she dropped the flowers in. She never arranged them, she liked to let the flowers choose their own territory, create their own personality.

"*Meow!*" Sasha was on the wrong side of the door.

Sally let her Siamese cat in and prepared a dish of salmon and sweet potato canned food, Sasha's favorite. Blue eyes met hers with a contented purr and using her silky body she rubbed against Sally's leg. They had been companions for ten years and had developed communication skills. This morning's leg rub said, "*thank you.*"

The aroma of morning coffee signaled the start of a new day. Last night's notes, from her adult-ed philosophy class, were on the table ready to translate from her in-class, unique shorthand to an easier to understand language. She enjoyed class discussions of ideas that were not always right or wrong. Life was so much easier when she kept her thoughts uncomplicated. Mornings were her time to slowly ease into a new day. The phone rang while she contemplated the length of her weekly things-to-do list.

"Good Morning," she said. And heard a familiar voice.

"Sally, it's Mary, I have great news!"

Mary Callahan's voice sang with joy across the airwaves. "Colleen called, they have their final approval. They're adopting a baby girl in China." A pause, a sigh, and then, "I'm gonna be a grandma! They're making travel plans, I'm going too." Mary began to ramble. Her words came in an unbroken flow. "My heart is racing. I'm scared. I don't know how to be a grandma."

"You will be the best grandma in the world." Sally was confident of her friend's ability to shower her granddaughter with love. She pictured a waving soap-suds bubble wand as she listened. Her mind wandered back to when they first met.

Sally had begun taking art classes at the community college. Mary exploded with happiness as she described her new painting. Her Irish blue eyes danced, and dark hair waved, unable to stand still she bounced up and down on her toes.

Suddenly, "Sally come with me!"

"China? Go to China? The other side of the world? It's a

different culture. I wonder if they speak English. At least most of the people in Europe understood English."

When Sally took a breath, Mary added, "We're going to Shanghai in September. They have incredible art museums, monasteries." And, the ultimate bait, "You can practice Tai Chi with experts."

Sally's hand shook. The phone became a foreign object. She took deep breaths. "You know I can't go anywhere in September. I need to be here with Michael. Walk the beach and remember the peace we had together."

"It's 2012, five years have gone by since the accident. It's time you stopped hiding. We always have fun on our trips. He'd want that. I know. He always planned happy times. Promise me you'll think about it?"

SALLY SAT ON HER SUN-ROOM FLOOR. NAVAJO FLUTE MUSIC played. A stack of China tourist information lay on her desk. She picked up a silver picture frame and held it in front of her. The handsome blue eyed, blond haired man smiled at her.

"What should I do? Should I go? I want to be here with you. I want to listen to the waves with you." Tears rolled down her cheeks. His face blurred. The blinding light returned, and she saw the car spin, the tree. It was the Ides of September 2007 again and her world was out of control. She woke in a hospital bed. Michael didn't. Her husband, her love, was in a coma and would never open his eyes again. He sleeps.

She touched her finger to her lips, then his.

"It's time. You must go."

SHANGHAI

SALLY

S ally's curls sang out, "Look at me!" as she bounced across the Shanghai airport. Her Polish heritage of blond hair, brown eyes and strong bones announced a visitor among a sea of small dark-haired citizens. Her confident stride concealed a nervous stomach and head full of, "What if's?"

Before leaving home, she went to the hospital to visit Michael and tell him about the trip, then walked on the beach to say goodbye. The ocean breeze touched her hands. She heard his heartbeat with each incoming wave. A quartz stone caught the sun, and she brought it home to add to their collection in the flower garden. His picture was tucked in her purple backpack. If she needed to talk to him, he was there. He would always be there to guide her on this journey.

The busy airport enveloped her, everyone was speaking a language foreign to her ears. Signs provided directions in strange squiggles. She was a seasoned traveler, but this was different. Her mettle would be tested.

Fifty-five was not too old for an adventure, she told herself. Reading about Shanghai's history had raised goose bumps on her arms. World history classes in school left out Japan's invasion of China, and newspapers in the '60s had little to say about the Cultural Revolution.

Her feet stopped and she made a 360 degree turn. All around her people moved with a purpose, their own lives. Now she had an opportunity to share this amazing culture. A push from behind woke her from her reverie.

"Move! We need to get a taxi." Mary waved a handful of Chinese dollars. "Look, Mao's portrait is on all the bills."

As their taxi approached the city, Sally sat spellbound. They zoomed past mile after mile of clustered condo towers emerging from fields outside Shanghai. The sameness of the complexes and absence of trees, flowers, or children's playgrounds reminded her of cave stalagmites. The towers outside were where much of the city's millions lived.

The taxi slowed to a crawl as they left the highway and joined cars, buses, trucks, mopeds and bicycles, all vying for road space. Horns called with individual sounds almost approaching a melody. Without street lights or apparent road rules, gridlocks stopped the taxi. Families of two or three on mopeds or bikes wove across the street. Sally marveled at the lack of road rage. There was an almost orderly movement in the midst of chaos.

Mary found a hostel for them. It was diagonally across the street from Colleen and Ron's hotel and a short walking distance to People's Park, a popular Tai Chi hangout. Sally was a practitioner. Tai Chi in China was on her wish list.

An odor of street exhaust fumes hit as soon as they left the air conditioned taxi. Hot cooking oil from a nearby sidewalk vendor introduced Sally to the country's perfume.

Once inside they collected a key, towels and a map to locate their room. On the second floor, the small room had two single beds. Each had a thin mat rolled up at one end and covered with a white cotton cloth. Open shelves were along a wall. A bathroom with a sink, western toilet, and shower stall was next door, and shared with another room. Clean and devoid of any decoration, this would be their home for the next ten days.

Sally's nerves tingled as she returned to the front entrance room. She was sleep deprived but excited and wide awake. A bar and bulletin board with hand written notes in English and Mandarin from people looking for travel partners were on a side wall. A second board advertised trips available through the hostel. Brochures from hostels in other cities and guided tours were in a stand. The friendly crowd socialized in English, Mandarin and a medly of languages from European countries.

"Come on, it's time to meet Colleen and Ron for dinner." Mary pulled on Sally's arm and they crossed an alley to the four-star hotel.

A gold carpeted floor and red silk drapes framed floor to ceiling windows. The hum of an air conditioner, to cool and purify Shanghai's polluted air, offered a welcome change from the stuffy hostel. First impressions of China were shared by the four travelers in the dining room.

"It's awful. The air is thick with street odors from cars and buses. The exhaust fumes must be unhealthy. My poor baby!"

Colleen had slipped into new mom mode as soon as her feet touched China soil. All she could talk about was the baby she was about to adopt.

"I think I can get some tools to tighten the slats on the crib in our room. It wobbled when I shook it." Ron's eyes searched the room for someone who could help with finding tools.

Sally studied the label on her beer bottle. "I can't believe the difference in price between bottled water and beer. Guess I'll be drinking a lot of beer. I can't tell what the alcohol proof is on this label, but it doesn't have much of a kick. I probably can handle more than my usual limit of two."

Mary held the dinner menu. "It's in English but doesn't make a lot of sense. I guess I'll ask the waiter what the people at the next table are eating. It looks interesting."

Colleen and Ron's adoption group from the states was having a get acquainted meeting after dinner. They would learn Chinese words to say to their children and receive the itinerary for the next week. They had appointments to visit the US Consulate to finalize papers for their child's passport. A visa was needed to leave China and enter the United States. And the baby was scheduled to have a physical exam. Time was set aside for shopping and family day trips.

Colleen's hands began to shake. "I'm scared. Do you think I'll be a good mom?"

Mary moved her chair closer to her daughter, "You will!" She covered Colleen's hands with hers, and smiled.

Sally decided they needed time alone and pushed her chair back to leave. "I think I'll go back to our hostel. I'm in the mood for bar food. This is a good time for you three to enjoy a family dinner, you'll be four soon."

It was dark outside and she was introduced to a new set of this country's rules. There were people everywhere: on the sidewalk, spilling out onto the street, moving in and out of store entrances. They stood in groups, talking and eating food from vendors selling barbecue, rice, and noodles cooked in woks over small fires.

The hostel residents were outside too. Young and old were partaking in the party atmosphere.

"Is this some kind of holiday?" Sally asked a young couple.

The man answered in a familiar Boston accent. "They do this every night. Chinese visit outside. The vendor food is really cheap. Try the chicken on a stick from the guy with the red umbrella. It's good." He pointed across the street to a cart with a barbecue grill.

Sally smiled, "Thanks, but I'll pass. I just got here today. I'm going to have a Ramon noodle bowl from the bar and get some sleep."

Her room was quiet, she was asleep before nine.

DINING WITH MARY THE NEXT MORNING, SALLY CHOSE AN American breakfast of scrambled eggs from the hostel's International Breakfast menu. There was English oatmeal, Swiss yogurt, and French pancakes. She was happy to see a fork arrive with her eggs. Bitter coffee convinced her drinking tea in China would be respectfully patriotic.

A guest book on a side table caught her attention. She leafed through pages with handwritten notes in English, French, and something else. A page of squiggles made her laugh.

"Mary, look, the Chinese don't have to worry about spelling. I don't think these symbols care. I always had trouble with spelling in school, still do. But now my computer has magic spell check."

"Somehow I don't think learning to write words in Mandarin is easier," Mary replied.

She planned to spend the morning with Colleen and Ron before they joined other new parents. The adoption group was going by bus, in the afternoon, to the orphanage two hours away. She told Sally she'd be back at the hostel for an afternoon ride on a sightseeing bus.

AFTER BREAKFAST SALLY WALKED TO PEOPLE'S PARK IN hopes of finding Tai Chi practitioners. Before she crossed the wide avenue, she stood on the curb waiting for a break in the constant flow of cars, mopeds and bicycles. The traffic in front of her didn't seem like it would ever end. People hurried across the street, but every time she started to step out something zoomed in front of her. She was turning and looking and mumbling about too many cars when two young girls smiled, said something in Chinese, and took her hands. They looked both ways, and, holding Sally's hands tightly, helped her cross the street. Sally thanked them, telling herself this was how she'd do it from then on. She'd just wait for locals, stand with them, and walk across the street when they did.

Sally was surprised to find paths divided the park into sections, each with an individual personality. She found a pond and benches in a tree shaded area. Another path led to a beautiful young woman in white silk performing BaGua in front of a bench with two older gentlemen. The girl moved in circles, bending and stretching, using her incredibly strong leg muscles to expertly perform a fast form of Tai Chi. She had seen BaGua on film, but never in real life.

After applauding, she spoke to the young woman. Her name was Lei and her parents lived in New York City. Lei spent vacations in New York and spoke excellent English. She had been demonstrating for her Tai Chi Master and his student from Australia.

Not wanting to pass up an opportunity to practice Tai Chi, Sally asked if she could practice with them. Lei asked her Master and translated that she should begin. Sally looked at the serene faces of the men on the bench and realized she was auditioning. With butterfly wings fluttering in her stomach she slowly raised her arms in the opening move.

When Master Quam stood to lead her, Lei, and his pupil in finishing a short form; Sally knew she passed inspection.

After they finished, Lei said, "My Master is famous teacher. I am his pupil for ten years. People come from many countries for his teaching."

Sally had practiced Tai Chi with a Master! A hope from before she left home.

"Please tell him I am honored to have had a lesson with him. You are a wonderful example of his success as a teacher. Thank you." Sally waved goodbye.

SHE LEFT THE SMALL GROUP TO CONTINUE ALONG THE PARK paths. On a secluded stretch ahead, a man practiced alone. She recognized his forms and stepped to the side to watch. He moved in a slow confident flow. An aura of peace seemed to surround him. When he turned and looked at her, he nodded. Sally felt an emotional pull to join him. She dropped her shoulder bag and stood behind him to copy his Tai Chi practice. He repeated the moves whenever she faltered with her attempts.

After the closing move the man walked over to her. "Hello, my name is Zhang Han." He spoke in careful English and gave a thumb up signal. "Good!"

Sally moved to pick up her bag and found they had both moved to the side of the path. Suddenly, she felt shy. He was attractive. She wanted to talk to him. "Thank you Zhang for letting me practice with you. I'm Sally Raymond."

He smiled, "I enjoyed you there. In China proper to introduce sur-name first. You call me Han."

Sally felt her face burning. "I just got here yesterday. I came with a girlfriend. I read about this park and hoped I could find someone here to do Tai Chi with." She was talking non-stop. What was the matter with her? She held her shoulder bag with both hands, as if it was a life line.

She looked into dark brown eyes with crinkly lines along their edge. His mouth formed a friendly smile. The gray in his short black hair added to her impression that he was a man of her age. There was a touch of sadness in his face. Maybe she recognized it because it matched her own.

He began to talk and explained he was an English teacher at a Shanghai school. He was dressed in a tan shirt and pants that fit loosely on his lean body, a typical Tai Chi practice outfit. He looked strong.

"Are you American?" he asked.

"Yes, I live in Massachusetts. She held up her right arm, bent her elbow, and dipped her hand down at the wrist to show how Cape Cod stuck out into the Atlantic Ocean. "I'm retired. I used to be a teacher. Now I walk on the beach, collect shells, and listen to the sea gulls." She described her garden, her home, the Canada geese, and her cat, Sasha.

"How do you teach English in school?" She wanted to learn about English classes in China schools.

"My school is for high school students. They study all day. School is their job. I teach English lessons on how to read and talk." He smiled. "You have good teacher, speak good English."

She recognized the friendly banter and answered back, "Thank you, I have been speaking English for over 50 years. I don't speak Mandarin."

"I speak Mandarin over 50 years. We have language in common." With some hesitation he asked, "Do you practice Tai Chi tomorrow? Shanghai has beautiful Botanical Garden. I can bring you. Would you like? There are flowers."

Sally noticed he had taken a step closer to her. His eyes studied her. A breeze ruffled his hair. His smile was tentative, almost anxious.

After a minute's hesitation Sally answered, "Yes. Han, that would be amazing!" They negotiated a time and place to meet, and Sally hurried back to the hostel. She had a date with a man in China! Not part of her trip itinerary, but it had felt right to say yes. She wanted to see him again and couldn't wait to tell Mary.

Tow hours later, while enjoying a lunch of beer and French fries at the hostel, Mary and Sally recounted their morning adventures.

"I met a man. I have a date with him." Sally announced with a shy grin.

"Of course, you do, you've been in China for at least 24 hours," Mary joked. "What kind of date?"

"He wants to take me to a park with flowers. I said yes, but I'm not sure if I should go. I didn't come here to meet a man."

"Do you want to go?"

"Yes. He's different."

Mary laughed. "He's Chinese, Sally. Not many Chinese men to date on Cape Cod."

"He lives here and I'm going home in ten days." Sally answered. "I don't know what I should do."

"This could be a good time for you. The reality is Michael is in a coma and you've been a widow for five years." Mary squeezed Sally's hand to emphasize her point.

"I know. The doctors tell me he will never wake. But I don't do well with relationships."

They sipped their beers. Sally looked at Mary and grinned.

"You win, I'll go on a date with Han."

Mary laughed, "I didn't have to do a whole lot of arm twisting."

A BIG RED BUS TOOK SALLY AND MARY TO THE CITY'S Pudong area, also known as New Shanghai. This had become the industrial area, on the East Bank of the Huangpu River, when Chinese architects were given a box of crayons and told to design anything they wanted. Or, at least that's what it looked like.

Sally stood under magical towers of glass and steel. The Oriental Pearl Tower stood on stilts to hold balls a giant might play with. The Jin Mao Building of 88 stories opened petals in stages as its flower rose to the sky. The Shanghai World Finance Center seemed to turn with the wind as its 101 stories rose to a top, with a hole provided for dragons to fly through. Hotels and businesses scattered their own playful glass towers along the riverfront.

She thought these giant towers looked like the children's playground missing from the stalagmite towers she'd seen the day before. She felt a heartbeat of joy seeing this beauty. If this was China's future, its strength was awesome.

The walkway along the river appeared to be a line of division. The water moved past today's wonders and carried away Shanghai's past. The area had been hit hard during the Japanese invasion of 1930.

"I learned practically nothing about China in world history classes in school." Sally said. "Han is a teacher, so I'll ask him. I bet he can tell me about Shanghai's history."

"Good idea. And you're thinking about him. That's promising." Mary smiled. "Lets go shopping and get something to eat."

They walked past street vendors demonstrating toys that flew, had wheels, and made noise. Mary stopped and examined each toy. She wanted to buy one of everything for her new granddaughter. Sally reminded her, "She's only one."

A jewelry store saleslady brought out velvet bags of pearls and explained how she would match colors and sizes for Sally and string the pearls for a necklace and earrings. Sally watched as holes were drilled in her chosen pearls and strung for a necklace using an intricate pattern of tying knots between each pearl. The finished necklace and earring set were perfect for a special occasion.

Feeling decadent, Sally suggested dinner at one of the fashionable restaurants on Nanjing Road. Mary found one on the next block. A handsome young waiter brought menus with pictures and chopsticks.

Sally asked, "Could you suggest something? We just got here from America and don't know what to order. I like what the people have at the next table."

"I bring fish and chicken. Very popular," the waiter responded.

Practice at home with chopsticks made eating doable with only an occasional use of fingers. Their food was delicious, but there were bones. Lots of bones! Every small piece of chicken and fish had a bone. Fortunately, they had enough napkins to hide them. Chinese restaurants on Cape Cod didn't serve chicken or fish with bones.

Sally exclaimed, "The cooks here need to go to Cape Cod to learn how to cook meat without bones."

"Do you want to explain to that nice waiter that you don't like the way they cook their food?" Mary answered with a grin.

"Maybe someone at the hostel can teach me how to eat around the bones." Sally was not finished with the bone issue.

MARY STOPPED IN FRONT OF THE HOSTEL DOOR. "I WANT TO stop in Colleen's hotel room. They're supposed to have their baby. She told me they expected to be back by 3:00. Will you come with me? I'm nervous."

Sally smiled. "Sure, but I won't stay long. This is a time for your family. Come on, I'll hold your hand."

Mary stood in front of the door to her daughter's room. She wasn't moving.

Sally asked, "Do you want me to knock?"

After a nod from Mary, Sally rapped twice, "It's us."

Ron opened the door to show Colleen sitting on the floor with a little girl in a white underwear shirt and pants. She had a pink bow on top of her head and short, jet black hair. Her tiny ebony eyes peered up at Mary.

"I put a bow in her hair so she would look like a girl. I put away the pink dress she had on and she doesn't have anything else to wear. We're going shopping tomorrow for clothes." Colleen held her daughter out to Mary. "Here's Grandma!"

Mary took a step toward the baby, then another. She took the child from her daughter's outstretched arms. Her face glowed. "I love you." Her first words to her grandchild.

"See you later." Sally backed out with a wave. And crossed the alley to the hostel bar.

SALLY THOUGHT THE CHINESE VERSION OF AN ENGLISH breakfast of oatmeal needed fruit. Warnings of "boil it, peel it, or forget it" left slices of watermelon as the only available addition to the sad gray mush. "Tomorrow I'm going to have a Chinese breakfast. This isn't working," she lamented and wrinkled her nose.

Mary wasn't eating either. She talked non-stop about her granddaughter. Describing how sweet she smelled, how soft her hair was, her perfect fingers and toes. "She fell asleep in my arms! She knows I'm Grandma, I can tell. I'm going shopping for baby things with them this morning."

"What should I wear to the park with Han?" Sally asked.

"You haven't heard a word I said." Mary scolded.

"Yes, I have. Your amazing granddaughter has ten fingers and ten toes. This is important, what should I wear? I go out to dinner or attend concerts with men back home for companionship, but I never want to share beach walks with them. Han asked me to share a walk with him and I want to go. I'm totally befuddled." Sally pleaded, "I need to decide something. All I have to wear are pants and tee shirts."

"Tie the lilac scarf you bought yesterday around your waist. Comb your hair, put on lipstick and smile." Mary chuckled. "Don't look so scared. It's just a walk in the park."

"Not funny. Let's decide on when and where we'll meet up later. There's a neighborhood tour at three. I saw it advertised on the bulletin board. It starts here." Sally had an anxious grin as she returned to their room for the scarf.

On her way to People's Park, Sally asked herself why she was so nervous. It was just a few hours with a man. She wasn't cheating on Michael.

When she arrived at the practice area, Han was waiting. He sprang forward with an eager, "Hello, I am happy you come."

After a brief awkward conversation about the weather, he patiently led her through Tai Chi forms. They seemed to be well matched. She stumbled with some moves and he paused to find the English words he needed. "This good. Stand straight. Slow. Be strong." Tai Chi was considered a martial art in China and had much more meaning than the "Its good for balance," description used in America.

Sally moved closer to Han as they walked down the crowded street toward the park subway station. She wasn't going to let him disappear and leave her alone in the middle of Shanghai. She felt in her pocket for her money and the card the hostel had supplied with their address in Mandarin. She could give that to a cab driver if she got lost.

Han took her hand on the walk down the stairs to the subway. His shirt sleeve slipped up to reveal a black mark on his wrist. It looked like a tattoo.

Sally was surprised to see a tattoo on a scholar and wondered what it signified. She liked tattoos on men with black leather jackets and motorcycles. She'd had romantic fantasies through the years of being a biker babe.

She was relieved when he stood close to her on the packed subway car. They were surrounded by people. Men standing close to her reeked of cigarette smoke. She coughed and leaned toward Han to sniff his shoulder. Thank goodness, Han did not smoke.

THE BOTANICAL GARDEN WAS BEAUTIFUL. SALLY BECAME aware of a softer side of China while she walked through gardens planted in intricate designs reminiscent of the delicate paintings and pottery she had seen in the shops. Birds sang, flowers filled the air with a garden fragrance. She relaxed.

Han bought paper bags of crunchy treats from a pushcart vendor. "Very Chinese," he said, offering a bag to her.

Brown pieces of some kind of nut tasted salty and had an exotic spicy odor Sally didn't recognize. They sat on a bench and ate the finger food; and watched children float boats and feed ducks in a pond.

"I read about the Japanese invasion of Shanghai. It's hard for me to comprehend living in a place during war. America has been at war with other countries and our young men lost their lives, but there hasn't been fighting on our land during my life. Battles were fought during the Civil War and much of the South was destroyed. Our country was divided. States in the north and south had different ideas about freedom. Sometimes families were divided."

Han's hand with a food tidbit stopped midway to his mouth. He looked off into the distance. His jaw muscles tightened.

"Oh, oh, what have I done? I said something wrong. What now? I shouldn't have tried a date. I'm terrible at relationships." Sally's mind raced.

Finally, Han spoke in a tight voice. "My parents told me about Japanese. I was child, do not remember. Bad time. Many people die. I am teenager for Chinese Cultural Revolution." His eyes took on a clouded cast. He shook his head for several seconds. "Bad memory."

"We don't need to talk about that. I'm sorry. I know so little about your history."

She was trying to think of something else to talk about when she spotted a Siamese cat. It left a group of children by the pond and walked toward them. It's long black tail stood straight up with a bend about two inches from the tip. Her cat, Sasha, home on Cape Cod, had the identical twist in her tail. The cat stopped in front of them. It sat and peered up with friendly blue eyes.

"*Meow.*"

"He say, 'I am happy you here.' in Chinese," Han translated.

Sally laughed, "She say, 'I am hungry, give me food.' in English." She leaned down to give the cat a piece of whatever it was she was eating. "My cat at home looks like this one. Her name is Sasha."

Han bent down to look in the cat's eyes. "Hello, Sasha, I happy to meet you." He stroked her back and smiled when she purred. She ignored Sally's offered food and wrapped around Han's legs.

Sally watched Han's transformation as he talked to Sasha in Mandarin, she seemed to answer him with more *"meows."* His voice became less strained, and he seemed happier.

When the cat returned to the children, Sally called out, "Thank you, Sasha."

Han got up from the bench, walked down to the pond area, and returned with a bag of seeds and two young men in military uniforms. "Man have food for birds. You like feed birds?" The young men were talking and Han translated. "They want picture of you. Blond hair people are special."

Sally reached up to fluff her hair. "Sure, I can do that." She posed with each of the soldiers while Han took pictures. The men talked some more and Han explained. "They want picture of you with me."

"I'd like a picture of us, too. I brought my camera."

When Han put his arm around her waist for the picture, Sally noticed they were the same height. His dark eyes seemed golden in the sunlight. His hands were small, but not smaller than hers, and they felt good on her waist. She felt comfortable with his steady gaze, friendly smile, and cheerful voice, and she wanted more.

After the photo session they walked among families of a

mother, father and one child. Parents held hands and formed a proud and protective link with their child. Fathers carried small children in their arms.

Blond photo posing continued as families asked her to pose with them. Sally wondered if adults would someday wonder who the blond lady was in their family pictures.

An outdoor restaurant with round tables and two chairs sent out an aroma of cooked food. There were round, wood boxes on a hot grill. The steam tantalized with an unknown fragrance.

"Tea and dumplings. You like?" When Sally nodded eagerly, Han led them to a table.

The tea menu looked similar to wine menus in America. Not having a clue what to order, she pointed. "I want this one," and used a confident voice, as if she had been doing this her entire life.

Han grinned at her choice. While he talked with the waiter, Sally looked at her chopsticks and said a little prayer that her food would not fall off.

Their tea arrived in tall glasses with whole tea leaves on the bottom. The water was very hot and Han instructed her to wait before drinking. He had ordered a different tea. After trying each one, she said, "I can taste the difference. Yours is stronger. Mine is lighter, minty."

"You have spring tea," Han explained.

The waiter brought a plate of dumplings that could easily be grabbed with chopsticks. Fortunately, there were no bones in the dumplings. Sally asked, "Why are there always bones in Chinese meat?"

Han smiled. "Fish are small, always bones; chicken cut, chop,

chop." Using his hand as a meat cleaver, he demonstrated. "More bones. It is proper to spit bones next to plate."

"Yuk!"

"Yuk?" he repeated, frowning.

"American slang. Means we don't have bones in fish and chicken."

The boneless steamed dumplings and tea were a wonderful treat.

"I think I saw a tattoo on your wrist. I'm surprised to see a teacher with a tattoo."

Han pulled up this shirt sleeve to reveal two Chinese characters. "Means strong." His fingers traced the tattoo. "I get in school when age 14. You have tattoo?"

"No. I hear it hurts," Sally grimaced.

Han smiled, "Young people have ink markings. Boys like dragons, girls like flowers. Some girls have dragons." His eyes twinkled in the sunlight. "Dragon popular symbol. For many years small mountain villages have special tattoos. Not so much today."

"I see lots of dragons. On jewelry, paintings, carved on wood plaques. I read the Han Dynasty was powerful. Why is your first name Han?"

"Han mean "*country*." My family one time from north country. Father say I remember where I from. You like to learn about China?"

"Yes, the more I read the more I want to learn."

"You tell me America. I tell you China." Han looked at his watch. "We start back. You go with your friend today, yes?"

As Han walked with her through People's Park, he asked if she would enjoy a boat ride on the Huangpu River to view Shanghai's skyline at night. "Very beautiful," he said, and asked if he could bring her and her friend the following night.

She said she'd ask Mary and giggled to herself when he walked her to the hostel door. "He's walking me home. Wait until Mary hears about this."

A young girl with round dark eyes introduced herself as "Fen," and began to lead the hostel group past small store fronts. Fruit and vegetables were laid out on blankets spread over the sidewalk. Sally looked at the forbidden fruit: delicious ripe grapes, peaches, and plums glistened in the sun. They beckoned to her. "Mary, see! The plums look so fresh, I'm sure they're clean. Don't you think one would be okay?"

Mary was taking pictures of smiling children, but she turned for a moment, "Remember, we have a date with Han tomorrow night. Do you want to take a chance on getting sick from that fruit? I read the boat ride is awesome."

After she pulled herself away from the fruit display, Sally followed Fen to a storefront with open barrels of rice. Fen explained, "Signs on barrel say where and when rice harvested. People have favorites."

Rice choices didn't seem so weird when Sally remembered the morning's tea menu.

Next were beans, peas, and bananas. "Hey! Wait a minute. I can peel a banana!" Sally exclaimed and handed two bananas to a lady with a small cash box. Then held out her hand with change and watched as her bananas were weighed on a hook attached to a hand-held cast iron balance scale.

"Mary, look, I've seen scales just like these in antique stores on Cape Cod."

Her bananas were handed over and a coin, carefully taken from her open hand. She peeled her banana and, with unnecessary flourish, began to eat her precious fruit.

The group passed boxes filled with eggs; small fish swam in ten-gallon metal tubs, mesh bags held live frogs. Food distributors rode by on bicycles with boxes and baskets with eggs and produce balanced on handle bars, or piled high behind the seat. They were able to weave in between road traffic and pedestrians without crashing. The street vendors didn't have refrigeration. The dozens of eggs loosely piled high were fresh that day and would be purchased by residents and cooks from the many neighborhood restaurants.

Small cafés opened onto the street, each with two or three small tables in front of the family's living quarters. Street vendors sold mysterious sandwiches wrapped in paper. The air smelled of hot oil in kettles ready for pieces of chicken to be dropped in and fried. Bargaining customers melded with the green, yellow, purple, and white colors of the fruit and vegetables, combined with exhaust fumes and unfamiliar spices the city street had a carnival atmosphere.

A restaurant front window displayed smoked birds hanging upside down. Fen explained, "People not cook home, home often room with many beds. Peking duck special meal. They bring duck to table, cut thin slices, show how to add meat, onion, carrots and sauce for thin pancake, roll up. Eat with fingers." She demonstrated holding an invisible roll in her hand and taking a bite.

Sally and Mary asked, in unison, "Are there bones?"

They laughed at having the same thought. Fen assured them, they would not have to deal with bones. A dinner of Peking duck sounded good.

Mary wrote a description of the restaurant on her travel-size note pad. She couldn't copy the name in Chinese. Not being able to read or write street and store names from Chinese characters made finding their way around the city a challenge.

When they returned to the hostel bar, Mary said, "I want to hear about your date with Han."

Sally smiled, "He isn't married. I asked. He's been a widower for three years. He dresses neat but casual and isn't at all stuffy. He has a tattoo."

Mary looked her in the eyes. "You do like him!"

Sally wrinkled her brow, "He's nice, but there's something he's not saying. He got visibly upset when he started to say something about the Cultural Revolution. It makes me nervous."

"Have you told him about Michael?"

"No. It's too complicated."

"Maybe you both have complicated stories. Maybe he's not perfect." Mary stated thoughtfully.

To change the subject, Sally raised her empty glass. "Kind of a good thing they have beer here since we can't drink the water. Another round?"

"Tell me about your granddaughter. What's her name?" Sally asked.

"They named her Hope and her middle name is Bridget after my mother." Mary answered. "I bought her a cute white romper outfit in Walmart, and a soft bunny. Colleen said I can buy more when we get home. They have a limited amount of suitcase space. She's a happy little girl."

Sally smiled at her friend, "Grandma looks good on you."

"It feels good. Colleen invited me to go with them tomorrow. The adoption group is going to a monestary for a blessing of the children. Will you be okay on your own?"

"Sure, I'll practice Tai Chi with Han in the morning. I want to take the red bus around the city. There's so much to see. We better get some rest now. I'm still not fully acclimated to the time change."

Mary nodded her head. "I agree. Let's hit the sack!"

SALLY'S AFTERNOON BUS CHOICE WAS AN HISTORICAL TOUR of Shanghai. She loved history. Ancient history lured her with its mystery. When she walked into the Pearl Palace, the serenity of silent monks praying in the monastery and the fragrance of prayer sticks wrapped her in a blanket of peace. Buddhism was older than Christianity and had survived China's war-torn history.

While wandering in the monastery, Sally remembered how she had railed against God when the doctors gave her the diagnosis . . . Michael was in a coma and would not recover. She hadn't been to her own church in five years, there was no peace for her there.

She knelt on a cushion, bowed her head, and put the palms of her hands together next to her chest. The golden Buddha, in a similar pose, smiled down on her.

A monk with a fringe of gray hair circling his head appeared beside her.

She took a deep breath, gathering the sacred incense into her lungs as she whispered. "It was dark, no stars. The only light was the flash in front of me. It was too bright. I couldn't see. I don't remember. The car wasn't there." She stopped to breathe. Another monk knelt down beside her. "I was driving. My husband, the man I loved with all my heart, is gone. Why am I here? Why did God leave me behind?"

She heard Michael's voice.

"I love you. You are where you are needed."

More monks surrounded Sally. The burning incense flickered out. Her watch indicated she had been there an hour, it had felt like a moment of time. Slowly she rose up, bowed, and said, "thank you."

The red tour bus sat out front, waiting to bring her to the next stop on her discovery trip.

The Shanghai Museum's round dome and square base symbolized a round heaven and square earth. It held ancient bronzes, ceramics, and paintings that dated back centuries. Sally walked the halls, read the visitor information cards, and got lost among the immense variety. Each Dynasty produced their own specialty and this museum had a wonderous collection of past treasures.

In Italy, European frescoes, mosaics, sculptures, and oil paintings had held her captive with their perfection. Today's museum stirred up fantasies in Sally's head about how it might have been for men to cast bronze, mold ceramics, and paint on rice paper scrolls.

Women envisioned pictures in silk and created wondrous

scenes with embroidery thread. Artists came alive when she stood inches away from their masterpieces.

She asked, "How did you do that?"

No one answered.

THAT NIGHT, SHANGHAI TOWER LIGHTS PAINTED A LIVING picture of modern art on the Huangpu River. The boat left ripples in the water that created a sense of motion along the waterfront. Colored lights twinkled, and left reflections that added another dimension to an entrancing landscape. Night tower images became paintings.

Sally turned to Han. "It's beautiful! I don't have words to describe how I feel right now. It's almost magical."

"I not have English words for, I am grateful to bring you here." Han replied.

Sally stood at the boat rail for the entire trip. Views on the return trip included industry in the making, more towers being built. She wanted to ask Han about the museum's art, where she could see more, but decided to wait. This night was for the city lights, its modern art.

After the boat docked, Han walked between Sally and Mary on the Bund's busy streets. The daytime cars and buses had been replaced with pedestrians and bicycles. The spicy aroma of food cooking on outdoor grills filled the air instead of vehicle exhaust. Night people were celebrating their freedom with laughter, friendly chatter, and food from the street vendors. Children ran taking and delivering orders. Music from radios played. Couples danced expert tangos in the street while onlookers encouraged them with applause. As one couple left, another entered the street "dance floor."

Han asked Sally, "Would you like to dance? Tango good, teach in school."

She shook her head, "I can't dance a tango. It doesn't look anything like a polka." As she watched the graceful couples glide along the street, she tried to remember if she had ever seen this on the streets of New York or Boston.

A bicycle bell dinged behind them. A girl rode by on a two-wheel bike with a golden retriever in her front basket. The dog held a pink ladies' handbag by the handle in its mouth.

Everyone seemed to know one another. Sally asked, "Do they meet here a lot?"

"People come every night. We visit on street. Homes are small, not space for many people. People come from country. Very poor. Work here, many jobs building." Han stopped and looked around. "Tell me about America. Where you visit?"

"We go to friends' homes. Some people live in big houses with many rooms and outdoor spaces for gardens. We cook and eat outside in the summer. Barbecue is popular." She saw his puzzled look and pointed at one of the street vendors, "Like that, for friends, maybe 6 to 12 people. People play games outdoors, throw a ball, gossip."

"Gossip?"

"Gossip is sharing family news. Talking."

Han stopped walking and turned, "Would you like to come my school? My students like conversation with Americans."

"Sure!" she exclaimed, then added a quick "Yes." Her slang seemed difficult for him to grasp.

"We go after Tai Chi tomorrow. You like?"

"Yes! I would like that."

"Why are all the people shouting, Han?" Sally asked, perplexed.

"Not shout, use tone. High and low tones change meaning of words. How you say word important." Han then said something, slow and clear.

"What did you say?" Sally tried to repeat his words.

"We begin return to your hostel." Han answered with a smile.

Did Sally imagine it, or was he walking closer to her? She felt his arm brush against hers as they traversed the crowds. Was that accidental or not?

After Han bid them good-night at the hostel, Mary stared at Sally.

"What? Why are you looking at me like that?" Sally asked.

"Just checking. I wondered where you went. You have a dreamy look."

Sally smiled. "It feels like today was a dream . . ."

DAYS IN SHANGHAI FLEW PAST, DELIVERING A SERIES OF LIFE lessons. Mary began learning how to be a grandmother, talking to a child who had only heard Chinese. Sally improved her Tai Chi forms and spent afternoons with Han at his school.

The high school was a two-stop bus ride from Peoples Park. An old stone building stood behind a cement yard with parked bicycles and mopeds. Han's classroom was on the 3rd floor reached by a staircase with narrow steps. Sally tripped the first time she used the stairs with her large feet and felt her face turn red when Han held out his hand to her.

His students called him "teacher" and clapped when he introduced Sally and told them she was an American and would talk to them in English.

Sally was nervous during her first visit, her hands were shaking. She glanced at Han casually leaning on his desk, and relaxed. Students hands waved with questions.

"How many in family? How many languages you speak? Tell about American government, democracy."

She kept her answers to textbook information on how the President and Congress were elected and the Declaration of Independence. Soldiers with guns outside the Communist government offices were a reminder to keep her political views to herself. When she visited the middle school, the children were surprised to learn English was the only language used by most people in the United States. English was taught throughout China, not as a second language, but for the purpose of international good-will. Everyone wanted to know if Sally had brothers and sisters. Sally's father had ten brothers and sisters. She had a brother who lived in Italy. How they had shared bedrooms, dining room tables, and family vacations made wondrous stories for the students. She enjoyed her time at the school more with each day she spent there.

At the park one morning Han said, "You like children, they like you. You good teacher. You can teach more, . . . if you stay in China." Han was careful with his words, it sounded to Sally that he wanted to spend more time with her. He still had not shared his past.

She said, "I like the children, I like the art I see in museums, and your culture. It's difficult for me to understand sometimes. I want to see more. There's a three-day trip to a city in the mountains I am thinking about going on." Sitting next to him on a park bench, her shoulder touched his. His body shook when he spoke. "I feel sad you leave."

She wanted to see more of him. But she hadn't told him about Michael.

"If I leave Shanghai will I see you again?"

"We send e-mail." Han answered with a bright smile. "I have friend in Yangzhou, school principal. I talk to him, maybe you teach there. Very pretty city on river."

LATER THAT NIGHT IN THE HOSTEL BAR, SALLY ANNOUNCED, "I've decided to stay in China for a while. I'm going to cancel my return flight. I'm not ready to leave, I want to see more. The people and crowded streets have grown on me. The hostel desk attendants have assured me they will find a good hostel wherever I go."

Mary smiled, "I'm not surprised. You've been beaming since we got here. In a way, I'd like to stay too. The art and history is addictive! But my granddaughter, Hope, is so wonderful I want to be with her. What are your plans?"

"There's a tour to Datong, a city in the mountains with a monastery and caves full of Buddhas. It's for three days and all inclusive, hotel, food, guide, even the bullet train from Shanghai." She showed Mary the brochure from the hostel bulletin board. "I'll leave my return plane ticket open, so I can stay until I'm ready to go home."

"You'll be careful, won't you?" Mary hugged her tight.

Sally pulled away and puffed out her chest. "Of course, I will. I can do Tai Chi."

After rolling her eyes and shaking her head. Mary asked, "Have you told Han you're staying?"

"Yes. He told me he was sad I was leaving so I told him about the trip to Datong. He suggested I teach at a school in Yangzhou. He's going to talk to the principal. Maybe I'll go there." Sally smiled, "Do you have any idea how long its been since a man told me he was sad we were saying good-bye? I really like him. Being here is so exciting."

TAI CHI FORMS AT THEIR FAVORITE PLACE IN PEOPLE'S PARK were taking longer. The unspoken message seemed to be that as long as they were doing Tai Chi, there wouldn't be a good-bye.

But the time had come. Han leaned close and brushed her cheek with a kiss. The kind of kiss teenage girls dream about. Except Sally wasn't a teenage girl.

She said, "Han I want a proper kiss. Be strong." Then held her breath, afraid she'd been too forward.

After a very long moment, his eyes sparkled, his shoulders squared, and with the determination of a Tai Chi master, he stepped forward, pulled her close, cradled her head gently, and kissed her firmly.

She felt his breath on her cheek, smelled the earthy aroma from his hands, and heard birds singing. Somewhere, birds must have been singing.

He moved his lips to her ear and whispered, "Not good-bye, Sally."

Sally looked into his dark eyes. His steady gaze matched his confident smile. She would see him again.

They walked quickly to her hostel. It was time to go to the airport.

THE PLANE TOOK OFF FOR AMERICA. SHE SAID HER GOOD-byes to Mary and Hope, and Hope's parents Colleen and Ron. With thoughts of love, she waved as the plane disappeared into the horizon.

She picked up her purple backpack, slung the straps over her shoulders, and walked toward the train station.

3

SHANGHAI

HAN

Han's classroom felt empty. The students were in their seats, the florescent ceiling light flickered on and off. He made a mental note to call maintenance, again. A white chalk message on his blackboard read, *Thank you class. Sally Raymond.*

There was a place in front of the class where Sally stood. His memory had marked the spot on the floor. He was standing next to her invisible shoe prints.

Sally left Shanghai less than 24 hours ago. He remembered kissing her. Her curls had tickled his nose when he whispered in her ear. She smelled like Lavender tea.

"When is the nice American lady coming back?" Han's students asked.

"She is not in Shanghai anymore. I don't know if she will be back."

"She is good teacher, tell her come back."

"I will tell her. Remember, talk in English."

While the students asked their questions Han remembered the day, only a week ago, when he first saw Sally. He had been practicing Tai Chi when she walked up the path leading to his practice area. She stopped, set her backpack down, and began to follow his moves. He had moved to the side of the path, so she could see him better and he could watch her. He slowed his moves, leading her.

He knew she was American right away. American women are independent. They travel alone. Her blond hair bounced. Her moves were stiff and awkward, yet she tried. So serious.

Tai Chi practice that day went on longer than usual, he repeated the moves. He was afraid she might leave when he finished the form.

"She tell us about America. Say Democracy vote for President."

"There are families with two, four and sometimes ten children."

"Atlantic Ocean has whales and big fishing boats."

The students had their own memories of Sally. She had drawn them out with casual questions about how they lived, what they ate, what games they played. Always smiling, she'd found a way to include each student in the discussion.

She talked to them about democracy, how it began with the American Revolutionary War.

Han's students didn't remember their own Revolution, the years without food. Mao had said people were power, make babies. There wasn't enough food and people starved. Adopted China-born girls lived in other countries. Boys in his school outnumbered the girls.

Han remembered his father and brother leaving, forced into the Army. He was 14 when he was sent away to school. The Red Guard were his friends. He went with them, he burned books and smashed family treasures. When it was over, there was nowhere to go, his family was gone. Villagers told him his mother and sister had moved away to find food. No-one had heard from his father and brother. Han had tried to find them, but there was nothing in Army records.

Tai Chi became his salvation. He found new friends, peace and strength. Tai Chi saved him during his youth, and again after his wife died. He wished there had been a child. Today he had his students.

"Do you want her to come back?" A question from a student brought him back to the present, away from his memories. Han did want to see Sally again. His friend, Frederick Werner, was the principal at the Yangzhou High School. They had a program for Americans to teach English in their schools. Sally might like that. He would talk to Frederick.

His friend answered the phone on the first ring. Frederick listened to Han's request. "I have an American leaving in three day's so she can teach here for a week. Now, tell me about this special lady. It sounds like she's important to you."

"My students loved her. She charmed the class. We spent some time together and, yes, I want to see her again. Don't act so surprised."

Frederick laughed. "Are you going to come too? My teachers want another one of your lectures on history. You captivate your audiences. Stay with us. Aimee will want to hear about your American."

Han sent an e-mail to Sally. He told her about Yangzhou, how she could teach school for a week.

He hoped she would agree to teach and he began to plan. A phone call to his school to schedule a substitute teacher for his classes. A talk in Yangzhou.

He often lectured on China's history; how the Emperors shed blood, Monks built monasteries, Japan invaded and slaughtered his people. How bad politics and lack of food had caused so many deaths. Yet lives were changing. Cultures isolated in mountains and deserts that had been separate for centuries were beginning to find each other. History was a good teacher.

Despite his own losses, Han loved China. He lived in its chaos and beauty. When he saw Sally again, how could he tell her how much his past hurt?

4

DATONG

SALLY

Scenery sped past Sally's window too quickly for her to comprehend seeing people or farms. Her eyes, brain, and stomach complained about the outside confusion. It was like being seasick on a whale watching boat when she wanted to watch the whales and her stomach had other ideas. The Shanghai bullet train's headlong dash to Beijing took only five hours to cover over 600 miles.

"Train go 350 kilometers. Very fast. Not good look outside," the elderly Chinese woman next to her said, seeing Sally's queasy expression.

The seat was soft, and when the back reclined, a leg rest rose. Sally closed her eyes, she had a long day of traveling ahead. The lighting in the car was dim, it was quiet. The train rocked her.

A gentle nudge from her seat companion woke her, "Welcome, Beijing."

The train was replaced by a plane and, later, a dirty old bus that made groaning noises when it struggled to climb the mountain.

The day's harrowing travel experiences ended in front of a hotel in Datong. Sally stood facing the Datong Hotel with its manicured garden. Her new friend, Alexandra Richardson, stood beside her, they'd met on the Datong tour bus. Alexandra explained the efficiency of China's travel vehicles during their ride from the airport to the hotel. Sixteen bus passengers joined them in the garden while their bags were unloaded.

"I really need a beer. Riding around hair pin curves on the wrong side of mountain roads, horn blaring with each blind turn, was beyond scary." Sally's voice was plaintive.

"The bus floor will never be the same. You stomped on your invisible brake for the past hour," Alexandra teased.

"My nerves are jumping. And my throat is sore from gulping air," Sally complained. "I hope they have a bar here."

"Four star hotels in China always have a bar," Alexandra reassured her. "This place will be a luxury after your hostel stay. Wait until you sleep on a soft mattress instead of a thin pad. The breakfast buffet will be amazing. Let's get a drink."

An expatriate from England, Alexandra lived in Beijing with her husband. She'd learned Mandarin and traveled while he worked at the Embassy. Also a fan of art, history, and beer, they bonded on the bus. After checking into their rooms, Sally and Alexandra met in the bar for the much-anticipated drink.

"What's life like in Beijing? Is it lonely?" Sally asked.

Alexandra sipped her beer and reached for the pretzels. "My husband works long hours and I miss him, but there's a huge population of expats. We have photography clubs, card clubs, and social groups. There are listings online for travel and a variety of classes. Anything you might be interested in is listed on the internet bulletin boards. Most spouses are not working and have an *Ayi* to help with housework and childcare. We have time to get together."

"An *Ayi*?" Sally hadn't heard of an *Ayi* before.

"The China government has a listing of women who will come in, do housework, and care for children. It doesn't cost much. Children often learn Mandarin from the *Ayi* and translate for their parents."

"Do the *Ayi's* cook?"

"My *Ayi* cooks occasionally. I have a stove and can make food from home. A stove with an oven is rare in China. An electric rice cooker, two-burner hot plate for steaming, and a wok is the usual."

"So, I guess *Ayi's* don't bake cookies?"

"Starbucks has cookies. Shopping malls are underground. The subways connect them. They have department stores with the latest European fashions and co-ops for international food. Sometimes you just gotta have a Hershey bar, even though it's expensive."

They ordered dumplings at the bar.

"What do you know about the China Revolution?" Sally tentatively asked. "I met a man in Shanghai, I think he was involved somehow. He got visibly upset when I mentioned the American Revolution and our Civil War. He started to say something about the China Revolution and stopped. I think whatever it is, it's significant." She remembered Mao was in Peking, now called Beijing. Alexandra liked history so maybe she would know.

Alexandra put down her beer and moved on her bar stool so

she could look directly at Sally and lowered her voice. "It was a huge turning point, the birth of Communism. How old is this man?"

"I don't know. I think around my age, late 50's. He has some gray hair." Sally responded with a shaky voice. She was beginning to think she might not like the answer.

"If he was a teenager during the '60s he may have been on a work farm or involved in the Red Guard. Children got involved at an early age. It was a brutal time. A lot of adults today want to forget. Some are ashamed." Alexandra paused, "Is this someone you like?"

Sally hesitated, "Yes, I think so. I'm not sure. I've only known him for 10 days, not long." She sipped her beer. "Why don't I know anything about this revolution?" Sally's stomach was beginning to tighten, her hand shook when she set the glass down. She began to wonder . . . "Do I want to know more?"

Alexandra spoke with conviction, "Probably because your country was at war in Vietnam. The Chinese were supporting Vietnam. America was an enemy."

"I remember when a lot of Chinese immigrated to America. My Tai Chi teacher came from China. He said he had to get out or he might have been imprisoned or killed." Sally looked at herself in the mirror behind the bar. Her head filled with memories of people she had known during and after Vietnam . Soldiers had returned home with post-traumatic stress. The mirror reflected her sad eyes.

Alexandra toyed with her beer bottle and ate the last dumpling. "The idea was for the peasants to follow Mao's teaching. Scholars were a threat and either left the country, if they could, or took a chance on the Red Guard destroying their books and property. Teachers and other professionals were sent to the country to be factory workers or rice farmers." She grabbed a handful of pretzels and crunched with resolve. "I have a friend in Beijing who lived through it. She's told me some sordid stories. She still has nightmares."

"I wonder if Han was involved. He seemed embarrassed. But he shouldn't be, it was a long time ago."

"I agree, my friend says she has to forgive herself. She was young and impressionable. She was positive she was doing the right thing for her country. When you get to Beijing, find yourself a copy of Mao's 'Little Red Book.' It'll help you understand why the Red Guard did what they did."

"All that violence sounds so different from the man I know. Han is a gentle, sincere teacher."

Alexandra took a last swallow of her beer. "I'd guess he is today. Let's go. I need to get some sleep. It's been a long day."

"I'm looking forward to a soft bed," Sally was ready for sleep.

THE SCREAM WOKE HER. SHE SAT UP. THE HOTEL TV screen was there, right in front of her. A bureau, her backpack on a chair, a window. A dream; it was only a dream.

Her cotton night shirt was plastered to her chest. The sheet had a wet sheen. Her heart was racing.

Sally took several deep breaths. She was in the hotel, safe. She had gone to her room, sat in bed propped up with pillows, and began to write in her journal. It had been a long day, so much to say, so tired.

The heat. Then the fire. The red flames reaching above her head, devouring the air. She gasped for breath and then she saw them. People were throwing books on the fire - chairs, tables, dishes that rang when smashed. An acrid smell. The children, Sally realized they were children. They were shouting at a gray-haired couple. The woman held a package of papers to her chest. A girl grabbed at the package. The elderly man put an arm out to protect his wife. A boy punched him in the stomach. Sally didn't understand the words, but she could see the hate in their young eyes.

Sally turned, tried to run. Her feet refused to move. Girls and boys raced past. The energy from the fire seemed to feed the children. They were everywhere, screaming.

Then she saw him. A teenage boy with unruly black hair, eyes that reflected the red night. He lifted an arm, his hand an open palm. "Stay away." His other hand held a length of metal pipe by his leg: Han.

Sally screamed.

THE 6:00 A.M. ALARM WOKE SALLY WITH UNFORGIVING loud peals. The tour bus was leaving early for a long day of sight-seeing. Last night's dream had not left her mind. The soft bed had not helped her sleep. She kept wondering about Han. Did he have a violent past? It scared her to think about it.

"Are you okay? Your eyes are red." Alexandra joined her at the breakfast table with coffee and a roll with butter. "They don't serve bread often at meals in China. It's always a treat to have a roll."

Sally's hands were still shaking. She held her tea cup gingerly, afraid she might drop it. "I had a nightmare last night about the Red Guard. It was so real. I still feel uneasy."

Alexander nodded. "Strange things happen in Datong. I've heard stories from visitors who heard and saw people from another dimension. One explanation is the altitude, oxygen deprivation can cause hallucinations. The one I like is there's a vortex energy opening here that allows visits into the past."

"I hope my next trip into the past, or wherever, is someplace happy. I need strong coffee." Sally wanted to fully wake up and put last night's past in the past.

"I'll show you where you can get some Americano coffee. You don't want to miss some of the breakfast treats they have here." Alexandra lured Sally over to the buffet tables.

ON THE BUS TO THE DATONG HANGING MONASTERY, Alexandra fiddled with her new camera. "I'm taking an on-line photography course. It's a little overcast today, terrific light for taking pictures. Some of my friends have done this trip and said when there is fog the temple halls seem to hang in air. I can't comprehend living on the side of a cliff even though I've lived in a London flat all my life."

"I know what you mean," Sally said. "I've visited Anasazi ruins in New Mexico and Arizona. Stone fortresses were built into mountain cliffs thousands of years ago. It took a lot of effort to bring stone and tree trunks from miles away. Then they were abandoned. They were very primitive. I always wondered how they kept children from falling off."

"Monasteries didn't have children." Alexandra added with a grin, "As far as we know."

"I wonder what living in a monastery was like?" Sally mused.

The bus pulled into a parking lot and tourists looked up. A series of rooms built on wooden stilts climbed the mountainside. With a fog rolling in, the monastery appeared to be suspended in mid-air.

Alexandra stayed behind to take pictures before climbing the mountain.

Impatient to see inside the monastery, Sally joined the other travelers. A narrow pathway wound upwards on the edge of the mountain.

A mist suddenly appeared and covered her for a moment. When the air cleared, she felt a breeze blow across her feet. Looking down, she saw old-fashioned sandals under the hem of a homespun cloth skirt. Her waist was tied with a rope belt. Long sleeves covered her arms. She was wearing a Monk's robe. "What had happened?"

Sally stopped and looked around. There was no one in front or behind her, the air swirled around. Her heart was racing, what should she do? She certainly couldn't continue to stand here. It was dark behind. A faint light ahead. A tentative step forward, and the mist, the vision – or whatever it was – disappeared. She continued the climb.

A whiff of burning incense escaped from the open door of a room ahead and welcomed her to enter. Colorful cushions were on the floor, small Buddhas sat on tables, and bamboo screens rested along the outside wall. The guidebook said the monastery had been uninhabited for hundreds of years. This room looked lived in.

A rustle behind one of the screens caught her attention. Sally looked down into a pair of bright blue eyes. A Siamese cat walked toward her.

She asked, "Do you see me?" An answering "*meow.*" The cat walked back toward the screen, stopped, and looked at her. "Do you want me to follow you?" Another "*meow.*" Sally bent down to pet the cat. "I have no idea what's going on but, okay, I'm coming. I'll call you Sasha after my kitty back home."

Sasha led Sally to an open deck with wooden benches that seemed to hang in space above a meadow. When Sasha sat, Sally sat too. She studied the world below, and saw a field of growing grain, chickens, and grazing donkeys. A stream ran across a rock floor. The road the bus had taken was gone, along with the tour bus. Buildings she'd seen in the countryside were also gone. The only people below appeared to be monks. They were working in a garden.

"Sasha, I think we've somehow traveled into the past."

The silence was absolute. If the monks were talking, she couldn't hear them. The wind didn't rustle through the trees. The air smelled sweet, clean, with just a hint of incense.

Sally sat in silence with Sasha. Soon her body began to relax. She decided to sit for a while in the peaceful atmosphere before going back down on the path to the tour group. Sasha's tail began to swing from side to side. Was it instructions? "*Pay attention, this is a lesson. Let your face feel the air. Hear the sounds of the earth. Enjoy mother nature's scents.*"

"Okay I get it," Sally smiled at the cat. "Solitude is not alone, stillness is not empty. Life is so much more than me."

Sasha jumped down and walked to a door at the far end of the porch. Outside the door stood a small wood table with a white ceramic bowl of water. Delicate blue and yellow flowers were painted on the inside and appeared to float on the surface. The cat drank the water and then sat.

"I would like a drink, Sasha, I'm thirsty too. But they told us not to drink the water in China."

Blue eyes shut and waited.

Sally looked at the bowl again. She really did want a drink. "I think you're right. If the water came from the stream below, it's safe to drink." She dipped a nearby cup in the bowl and drank the sweet cool water. She wondered how it stayed cool.

Sasha led her inside. They were in a room with six monks sitting cross-legged on bamboo mats in front of a tall golden Buddha. There was a low murmur of chanting voices. Sally looked down at their bald heads, and gasped. Her hands flew to her head, and she let out a sigh of relief when she felt curls. After she tucked her hair behind her ears and pulled up the hood she smiled at Sasha. "That was a close call, I don't plan to be here long, I want to keep my hair."

Sasha growled, her eyes narrowed in warning slits. Sally knew that meant, *"Be quiet, move along."*

As they walked down an inside hall and up a few steps to the next room, she whispered, "Thank you for your prayers," to the monks.

The next room was a work room. Four monks were sitting at tables with pieces of rice paper, brushes, and small dishes of colored ink. The monks were grinding different colored minerals with a stone pestle. Then they added water to make a pallet of hues. They painted flowers and scenery on the paper in front of them. Human hair brushes were moistened and twisted in their mouths to form broad or sharp points.

Sally walked behind the monks and looked at each picture. She marveled at the delicate painted landscapes that were similar to those in the Shanghai Museum.

Finished pictures lay on tables to dry. Some hung on the walls. Torn rejects with smudges littered the floor. Having discarded many unfinished paintings, she could relate to the frustration felt by the artists. She wanted to sit down and paint with them, but Sasha started for the door.

After a sigh Sally turned to leave. She liked watching the artists. "I'm coming. But sometimes you're not fun, Sasha."

"Meow!"

The stairs had been made for smaller people with smaller feet. Steps were narrow, and her size 9 shoes overlapped each tread. The risers were too short. Sally had to be careful not to stumble. The monastery had a lot of stairs connecting its many rooms. She stopped for a moment to catch a breath of air and thought about the old monks who climbed these stairs daily.

Sasha climbed the stairs with an easy bounce on each step.

Sally followed into a room without walls on three sides. It was an open pavilion with screens that could be moved to form private meditation areas. She sat cross-legged on the floor and was surprised her legs could still bend under her. It had been years since she had sat in the lotus position. When she looked at her feet she found a small piece of paper with a slightly smudged hand-painted flower wedged into one sandal. She had unknowingly collected a discard. Holding the monk's painting, she spent her alone time in meditation. Soft fur brushed her arm. Blue eyes reminded her she was not alone.

More stairs and then a choice. Off to her right, a hallway led to a cluster of small rooms. In front of her, a step into a larger room. The rooms to the right might be the monks' private living quarters. She followed Sasha into an amazing place of worship that seemed to be sitting on top of the world. Lights twinkled overhead, lighting the room like a blanket of stars. A pool in the middle of the room was surrounded with elegantly stitched cushions.

Sasha walked over to the pool, then came back and looked up at her. Sally didn't follow her.

"I don't want to go there. I've read about looking into a pool and seeing your future. I want to keep mine a mystery." She circled the room, admiring the paintings on the walls.

The watercolors appeared to tell a story about Buddha. The painting to the left of the door showed a young Buddha dressed in an embroidered robe and wearing long gold earrings. The next pictures looked like a rich palace. Then there were thin people with a dark background. Buddha then began to wander in landscape paintings. The last painting on the right side of the door showed Buddha seated in the lotus position, wearing a simple robe and his ever present serene smile. Sally remembered the Daoist belief was about Buddha's enlightenment and reaching transformation.

Sally lost sense of time. When Sasha rubbed against her legs she jumped, startled. She looked around her one more time before following Sasha down a set of stairs along the outside of the monastery rooms. They ended their downward journey at the walkway Sally had used to enter the building.

Sasha stopped at the door and sat down. Ahead, on steps leading downward, a gentle breeze blew a mist of dancing air.

With tears in her eyes, Sally said, "Thank you, Sasha. I wish I could take you with me, but you belong here. I'll remember our tour." She walked into the mist.

In a moment her feet became heavy with walking shoes. Her

legs were encased in cargo pants, and below a busload of people were yelling and waving their arms. "Hurry up!"

On the bus, Alexandra asked, "Where were you? I looked everywhere."

Sally smiled. "I found a cat and went on a tour with her."

Alexandra opened her mouth to say something, apparently changed her mind, and closed it. After a moment she said, "I took some great pictures. The view from up there is fantastic. Did you see the paintings on the walls? I think it's amazing how they were able to draw and paint such delicate flowers."

"Yes, the monks were terrific artists. Makes me want to paint the flowers in my garden at home."

Alexandra nodded. "Me too. If you're interested, there are Chinese painting classes in Beijing. When you get there you can take a class. I'll fix it for you."

"I would like that! I don't know when I'll be there, maybe in a couple of weeks?"

She leaned back in her seat, closed her eyes, and replayed her visit with Sasha. Had she really gone back in time? She remembered each room, each Buddha, the monks painting, the mysterious star filled room at the top. Was it a dream? Or a vortex? Whatever it was, the time with Sasha had given her a wonderful memory of her visit to the monastery in the clouds.

BACK AT THE HOTEL SALLY HURRIED TO HER ROOM. AFTER closing the door, she opened her left fist. Lying in her palm was a scrap of rice paper with a delicate, slightly smudged, hand-painted flower. She carefully wrapped the treasure in a tissue and tucked it safely away in a pocket of her purple backpack.

BEFORE GOING OUT FOR DINNER, SALLY CHECKED HER E-mail. A note from Mary included a picture of Hope in a playpen with a white bunny from China. Sasha sat outside the playpen. "We are still exhausted but happy to be home. It's only three days and Hope is adjusting fast with Sasha's help. I brought your cat to Colleen and Ron's house, and Sasha stays with Hope all day."

Sally smiled. She had spent the afternoon with a Siamese cat. And there was Sasha on Cape Cod.

An e-mail from Han remained unopened. Her stomach clenched. Rubbing her head, she ruffled her curls and stared at the computer screen. *"He doesn't know about the dream."*

She took a deep breath and opened the e-mail. "I tell my friend in Yangzhou you are good teacher. Children there will be happy to talk English. I give him your e-mail. Very pretty city, I hope you go. I hope I will see you again."

Another e-mail, from Frederick Werner, Principal of Yangzhou High School. "My friend Han say you make his students happy when talk English. I invite you to come to Yangzhou as our school guest for one week. Speak English to our students. We will have honor for you to be here."

The German name was a surprise.

She wondered about that.

There were instructions on how to get to Yangzhou and how to reach Frederick. Sally made a fist, raised it and pulled down. "Yes! Next stop, Yangzhou!"

SALLY AND ALEXANDRA JOINED THEIR FELLOW TRAVELERS for a buffet dinner. Groups of six sat at large round tables with a lazy susan in the middle. Ten to fifteen plates of food were on the turntable. There were round plates with green vegetables, hot tin plates with pieces of fish, chicken, and sweet and sour pork. Each dish was attractively garnished.

The Chinese members in the group demonstrated how to use chopsticks to take small servings from the turntable and put them on dinner plates. They pointed with chopsticks at the dishes that would be near them soon. A fish dish seemed to be a favorite. Sally was waiting for it to arrive in front of her, but it emptied two diners before her. She scowled. Another fish plate came around, but she could see bones. She reached for a round piece of meat instead. It looked pretty on a flowered plate.

"That's either snake or eel," Alexandra cautioned. "It's considered a delicacy." Alexandra's warnings of, "That's going to be hot, I can see seeds," or, "that fish has tiny hair like bones," saved Sally from making wrong choices.

Dinner continued while dishes kept arriving. When the food changed to sweet tidbits and the ever-present melon slices, Sally knew it was almost time for a beer at the bar.

Seated side by side at the hotel bar Alexandra said to Sally, "So, are you going to tell me about the cat?"

Sally wrinkled her forehead. "It's hard to explain. Kind of personal." She paused. "The cat lives in the monastery."

After an exasperated sigh, Alexandra said, "Okay. Good thing Brits are told to be kind to the Colonists." She changed the subject. "I'm excited about going to the grottoes tomorrow. The caves get four stars on the expat bulletin boards."

"I read that the caves were not naturally formed in the

mountain. They were dug by hand. They didn't have steam shovels. I'm trying to picture how they moved the earth away from the mountain to make a cave." Sally looked at her hands, pink and soft. No calluses. "I think it would hurt."

"It wasn't *a* cave, it's 252 caves with 51,000 Buddhas." Alexandra sighed. The numbers were overwhelming.

"At home, I dig in my flower garden, sometimes pile rocks to make a tower, and work at it all summer. The guidebook says in 400 something AD it took them about 40 years. Forty years goes by fast. I'm 56 and can clearly remember when I was 16."

Both women chuckled over 40 years flashing by them.

Alexandra announced, "I think this is a good time for us to retire, and get our beauty sleep."

AFTER LING INTRODUCED HERSELF AS THEIR TOUR LEADER, the driver pulled onto the highway in front of the hotel. Another frightful ride on narrow roads followed before the bus arrived at the Yungang Grottoes, at Wazhou Mountain. Before climbing off Alexandra leered at Sally and asked, "Do I need to tie a bell to you today? Is your watch working? Remember, we're here for only three hours."

Sally gave a playful shove. "Go do your camera thing."

Alexandra joined the photographers looking for the perfect spot to take the perfect picture. Sally strolled the half-mile stretch of sandstone caves. She marveled at a two-story Buddha and posed for a blond photo with a young couple. She followed visitors into two caves and moved around the inside rooms with writings and delicate carvings of Buddhas, farmers, and animals on the rock walls and ceilings. It was amazing. She wondered what was in the other caves. There were so many.

Buddhas were everywhere, each with his own serene expression. Sally pressed her index finger to the middle of her forehead where the Buddhas had a teardrop bump. That represented a third eye. Buddha existed beyond time and space. His long droopy ears evolved from the heavy jewels worn in his earlobes in his earlier life of wealth. He had reinvented himself and gained serenity. Sally remembered the monastery paintings from the day before and tugged at her earlobes to gain her own enlightenment.

The Buddha's hands held messages called *mudras*. Holding her hands in front of her, Sally imitated them: Palms out, fingers up, meant protection. That made sense; it was something people did naturally in order to show "stay away." The giant Buddha hands with thumb and fingers touching, meant teaching. The statues with hands cupped in their laps were meditating. The Buddha with his hands together against his chest reminded Sally of her time at the monastery in Shanghai. Michael had given her a message there. She pressed her hands together and felt warmth travel from her palms to her heart.

A group led by a local guide arrived. Sally listened to the woman, dressed in a bright yellow blouse and pants, explain: "The caves were dug from the top down so they could easily cart away the dirt. Inside some caves, stories are told on the walls. I played on the Buddha statues as a child. Now that Datong has grown as a tourist center, many caves are roped off to protect delicate statues."

"So that's how they did it!" Sally said out loud. The question of how the caves were dug had plagued her all day.

A teenage girl with a cooler was selling bottled water. A

bench under a tree looked like the perfect spot to drink and relax for a few minutes. As she sipped the cool water, Sally wondered what life was like in the 5th and 6th centuries. Religious life must have been paramount for people to have made such an enormous tribute to the Buddha.

A chilly breeze left prickles on her arms. Deep breaths and hands cupped in her lap slowed her heart. Behind closed eyelids, Sally let the tourists disappear. In their place, an army of small men climbed ladders, chiseled rock, and drank water from buckets brought by children. The sound of tapping stone on stone matched her heartbeat. Drifting cave dust gently fell at her feet. The building of the caves was peaceful, a meditation in itself.

A bright flash of light made Sally open her eyes. Alexandra stood above with a triumphant grin. "Got it! A perfect picture of an American tourist napping at an historic monument in China. Time for us to leave."

"Be nice or I'll tell the Queen," Sally joked and followed her to the bus.

WHILE THE BUS DRIVER MANEUVERED AROUND PARKED CARS and out onto the road again, Ling announced. "We're stopping at more caves in a village near Datong. These are called 'Farmers' Caves.' The Yaodong people were farming clans that lived in mountain caves about 18,000 years ago. Around 4,000 years ago, they moved away from the mountains. They built attached dwellings of sod, wood, and rock in the shape of caves with a single door and one window. There are villages that have been lived in for thousands of years, and we can visit one on our way back to the hotel."

Sally watched the landscape change from mountain to valley, and told Alexandra, "I don't see any farming, just a lot of mud. There isn't much green around here."

The bus stopped at a village of small round-topped buildings. "Where are the barns?" She asked her companions, who responded with shrugs.

A boy and girl dressed in blue and pink jackets watched the strangers get off the bus. They were young, maybe four or five. "They look like Navajo children," Sally said. "In fact, this could almost pass as a Navajo village. See the homes over there? Hogans are built with dome roofs too. The only difference is hogans are made of adobe or wood and are not attached to each other. Navajo families live miles apart on the reservation. They raise sheep."

Alexandra was in photo mode. "I'll take pictures for you. Get close to the children and smile."

The tour group walked down a narrow, muddy lane. A man was digging what looked like a well. A donkey stood nearby eating dry cornstalks. "It smells like a barnyard. All we need is some chickens and I'll feel it's a real farm," Sally looked from right to left, taking in the rural scene.

"Over there, on the hill." Alexandra pointed out a flock of chickens pecking at something on the ground.

Sally smiled. She enjoyed seeing the farm life after spending a week in Shanghai's crowded streets.

They passed a dome-shaped building with a front porch. Two dirty bicycles leaned on a wood rail. Two men stood near the bikes, smoking cigarettes. They wore gray cotton shirts and pants, with bright red and green knit scarves wrapped around their necks. As the group passed, they followed the strangers with their eyes. Sally guessed tour groups stopped here occasionally, but visitors were rare. She wished she could talk to them. Her father had come from a farm in Illinois.

The dirt lane ahead passed through more fields and ended in a Y. The lane to the right had a row of about ten round-topped homes with doors opening onto mud. With a little stretch of her imagination, Sally saw the resemblance between the mountain caves and these dwellings. The guide veered to the left and the group followed. Soon they walked into a square surrounded by a low rock wall. On one side was a paddock with a roofed shed. Donkeys were eating hay or straw.

"It's the barn. Look, Alexandra, there's a horse, too!"

Sally's heart beat with an extra tremor as she watched the donkeys eat; smelled the barnyard odor and felt the mud squish under her shoes. She thought about her father and America. A wave of warmth engulfed her. There was only a moment to stand, look, and remember home.

"I'll take a picture for you, but then we need to join the group." Alexandra positioned her camera so she could get a shot of the barnyard and Sally's wistful expression.

Inside a cave the group was introduced to a man sitting on a platform bench under the only window in the dwelling. He welcomed the guests into his home in Chinese, flashing a confident, toothless smile. A cotton shirt and pants revealed a lean, well-muscled body. His two rooms were attached to a row of five homes. The entrance room held storage for clothes, gardening tools, and water pails. Colorful pictures hung on the walls. A second room of approximately 10 by 20 feet had a chair, a table, and a small cooking stove with a wok and tea kettle. The large platform bench where the smiling owner was perched served as his bed. Ling explained, "This called a *kang* and his sleep platform at night. During the day a sitting bench."

The guide also pointed out, "There isn't electricity. The cooking stove have space under for fire. Pipe from under stove go under sleep platform. Keep warm in winter."

Sally touched the pad. "It *is* warm. I bet the thick rock walls keep the rooms warm in the winter and cool in the summer."

Community water came from an outdoor well pump. The village shared the courtyard and fields. Mud was everywhere. Mud-caked bicycles leaned against walls. Everyone wore rubber boots.

On the way back to the bus, the group was invited into the village store. The first room of the two-room dwelling contained sealed packages of mystery food, several long shelves of alcoholic beverages, and, on a counter, a very large piece of thawed meat.

Sally asked "Is this meat for someone's dinner tonight? What is it?"

Ling questioned residents on the porch. "They make shopping trips to town. Van take them. I not know what meat is, maybe from hunting trip. About 40 people live here, meat dinner for village."

The second room next to the store appeared to be the neighborhood meeting room. Women sat on the *kang* and played Mahjong. Mahjong players on the tour immediately grouped around the players and watched several plays. They agreed with each other that the game pieces were not the same as the ones used in the United States and England.

The village visit lasted a little over an hour. Curious residents wandered down the mud path to the bus to pose for pictures and wave goodbye. Some wore polyester jackets. Little else had changed in this community in thousands of years. The friendly people living there today were at home with their ancestors.

As the bus left the village, Sally remembered the long rows of bottled booze on the store shelves. Maybe there were some changes after all.

AT AN OUTDOOR MARKET SALLY'S ARMS WAVED IN CIRCLES encompassing the bedlam ahead. "This doesn't look anything like Stop-n-Shop."

Alexandra shook her head. "This is China. A lot of people live here." She raised her eyebrows and gave Sally a nudge forward.

The market was the last stop on the day's tour of historic Datong. Sally hesitated, the crowd ahead was loud and the air was thick with unknown odors.

"Come on, I'll give you a tour. My *Ayi* brought me to a Beijing street market once. It's just a really big farmer's market."

"I asked Han about food stores. He planned to take me to a market but we didn't have time."

"You talk about him a lot. Do you think you'll see him again?"

"I might see him in Yangzhou. He helped me get a job teaching there for a week. If he can get time off, he will be there too. I hope so, I don't know anyone else there."

Alexandra grabbed her friend's arm. "I hope so too. He sounds like a great guy. For now, let's go and see the food vendors. It looks like I get to have the pleasure of showing you how to shop Chinese-style. Come on, we'll start in the produce department." Alexandra headed down the first row of tables, Sally in tow.

Long wood tables held a large assortment of green and yellow vegetables arranged in front of women with hand held scales. Shoppers picked up beans, squash, bok choy, and handed them over to be weighed. Cash was tucked away in wooden boxes or cloth bags, and the purchased food put in the buyer's mesh bags. Melons, bananas, small fruit similar to plums, and grapes, were near the vegetables.

After purchasing a bunch of bananas, Sally peeled one and took a bite with a contented smile.

In the meat department, Alexandra turned to Sally. "This is very different than American or English butcher shops."

Live chickens and ducks were in cages. A woman walked past holding a chicken by its legs, its wings flapping. Dead chickens, without feathers, and boiled, were on tables, heads and feet intact. A side of beef hung from a hook. A man stood with his machete, ready to slice off a hunk. Buyers seemed to be ordering specific cuts and weights. Chunks of meat sat on tables for shoppers to pick up, examine, and put down if not satisfied. Conversations between the customers and the butcher were lengthy.

Alexandra explained, "They're price-bargaining. It's considered a national sport."

Sally grimaced, "Let's move on. I never thought about pork chops or steak any way but plastic-wrapped." She was uneasy seeing live birds and unrecognizable hunks of meat. The lack of sanitation bothered her.

They passed by swimming fish, live turtles, and frogs in pails of water. The seafood department wasn't any better and Sally kept walking.

A boy sat among boxes of candy eating a piece of sugar cane. He hacked off an end with a small machete and sucked at the sap. Finally, Sally thought, we're in the dessert department. There were candies wrapped in paper and small balls of steamed dough. She didn't see cakes, cookies or pies and decided to buy a bag of paper-wrapped candy.

A take-out dinner kiosk consisted of a huge pot of boiling oil and dead chickens hanging from hooks. Sally watched a shopper chose a chicken. The chef dropped it in the stinky oil, pulled it up, looked, and dipped it again. When cooked to perfection the chicken was placed on a wood board. With a machete and speed and precision, the chef turned the chicken into a pile of pieces with a bone in each one.

Alexandra said, "I don't go to the market. I give my *Ayi* a list."

Sally looked down the street at all the food stalls. Dirt and dust filtered through the air. Salesmen called attention to their wares with bells, whistles, and colorful flags. "I'm glad I don't have to cook. It's best to eat out and let food origins be a mystery."

THE BARTENDER SET TWO BOTTLES OF BEER IN FRONT OF Sally and Alexandra.

"I'm going to miss this girl-time when I get home. Expats tend to be chaperoned in Beijing. There is an image to uphold. Our apartments are too small for comfortable gatherings and the local bars are either too seedy or too sophisticated." Alexandra picked up her bottle, "Here's to good memories."

Sally raised her bottle and they clinked. "I plan to visit Beijing. Any chance I can see inside your Embassy?"

Alexandra's eyes brightened. "I'm sure my husband could arrange a tour. Do come! I'll find art classes for us and we'll eat at local hangouts. You might be ready for some American food."

Sally smiled at the thought of a hamburger. She thought of Mary while daydreaming about food from home. "I have a friend on Cape Cod who would probably turn cartwheels to get into a British Embassy. If I e-mail her tonight she might decide to come back. Will two visitors be okay?"

Alexandra pretended to frown. "If she's another 'Yank' like you, it might put a bit of stress on the English gentry."

"Mary will bring a proper dress and she'll even curtsy. She just became a Grandma. Her daughter and son-in-law adopted a little girl in Shanghai. It's possible she might be ready to take a break from her grandma-spoils-a-baby duties. She told me she wished she could have seen more of China before she left."

In her hotel room, Sally read an e-mail from Mary extolling the wonders of her perfect granddaughter. She typed a reply. "I have news for you . . ."

Then an e-mail to Han. "Datong is fabulous! I met an English expat from Beijing. She invited me to visit. Tomorrow I leave for Yangzhou. I miss our Tai Chi practice."

Her mind began to drift. A familiar warmth wrapped around her chest. She looked in the mirror over the dresser, and asked Michael, "Were you at the Farmers' Caves today?"

"You brought me there. You can let go of me."

"I can't. Not yet."

Sally stared at the reflection of her sad eyes. Michael was silent.

BEFORE BOARDING THEIR SEPARATE BUSES, SALLY GRABBED Alexandra in a strong hug. "I'll see you soon."

Alexandra held tight. "You're a terrific ambassador for America. I want to visit you on Cape Cod."

YANGZHOU

SALLY

Frederick's e-mail instructions on what train to take for Yangzhou, along with a copy, in Mandarin, were in Sally's pocket. She showed these to the conductor in Datong before boarding. He smiled, carried her backpack and led her to a window seat near the back of the car.

A whistle blew, and the train rolled forward. After two hours, the conductor brought her a bottle of water and a package of meat rolls. "Good!" he said.

The savory roll was delicious. She nodded and smiled her thanks. Tense muscles in her neck and shoulders relaxed. She felt safe. Later, when she needed the bathroom, she discovered he had placed her at the end of the car with a Western-style toilet.

UPON ARRIVAL IN YANGZHOU, SALLY STEPPED OFF THE train and stood on a platform looking around. This was her first time on her own in China, without a group guide or girlfriend fellow traveler. Not able to understand signs or the language, she stood still and watched everyone around her. People moved toward the two exits. But she was afraid to move. She didn't want to get lost.

The Yangzhou High School had promised she would be met at the train station. She put her purple backpack down in front of her and hoped someone would see her blond hair. Passengers looked and smiled at her, but everyone kept walking. Minutes seemed like hours.

Suddenly, a familiar voice came from behind. "Hello, Sally. Welcome to Yangzhou."

"Han!" She turned and grabbed him for a strong hug. Han was here! She was not alone. "I didn't know you would be able to meet me. Your last e-mail said you were trying to come. What a wonderful surprise! You're here!"

"Someone tell me Americans like surprise." With a wide grin he grabbed her backpack and took her hand. With expert crowd control, he led them through the waves of incoming and outgoing passengers and up a set of stairs to the street. Her backpack was quickly put in the trunk of an idling car. They climbed in and the car sped into the stream of traffic.

Sally was seated in the front seat next to the driver, who introduced himself. "I am Frederick Werner, Principal at Yangzhou High School. We are grateful you will teach our students English. They are happy for American conversations."

"I'm retired and I don't have any type of teacher's certificate with me. Is it going to be permissible for me to teach?" Sally asked.

"It is important for students to speak English. American-

English is good. Our country wants international language. We have approval for one week visitors for our school,"

"Did you have good train ride?" Han asked, from the back seat. He leaned forward and put his hands on the back of the front seat close to her head. When Sally turned to talk to him, he was close enough for her to feel his breath on her cheek. It felt natural to put her hand on top of his. After several moments of looking into his eyes, and with a slight stutter, she said, "It was a good ride. The conductor was great. I think there was something in the Mandarin letter from the hotel that helped."

Han's hand turned over and was holding her hand.

A conversation took place between Frederick and Han in Chinese. Han blushed.

"What?" Sally asked Han. She started to giggle, it was funny to see his face turn pink.

"He say you pretty American."

Frederick grinned. "I tell him he looks happy. American lady is special. We are friends for long time. I like to see him happy."

Sally felt her face grow hot. "Okay, boys, thank you for the compliment. But please, no more Chinese in front of me." To change the subject she added, "Frederick Werner doesn't sound like a Chinese name."

"My father was German. When a young man he come China to teach, found my mother. She have family here and they stay. He want me to always remember my European heritage. My two sisters have Chinese names, Huiqing and Xiaolian. Our teachers will help you with students' names. Sally is unusual name for us. You can help us with American names."

Sally nodded. "I will. I'm excited to spend a week here. I want to live like a local."

"We would like you come to get acquainted dinner tonight." Frederick rolled his r's a little, reminding Sally of friends from Germany.

The train station was an hour's drive outside the city. They began to pass clusters of bleak housing towers similar to those she had seen outside Shanghai and Datong. As they approached Yangzhou center, mopeds and bicycles joined cars, buses, and trucks with their loud horn signals and exhaust fumes. Frederick parked in front of a downtown hotel.

Han carried Sally's backpack into the lobby. He gave the desk attendant a card and handed her a room key. He lingered, shuffling his feet, then put the backpack down. "The teachers look forward meeting you for dinner. I'll be back at six to bring you. Is that good?"

Sally smiled. She wondered why Han appeared so awkward. "Great. I'll unpack and rest."

She grabbed her backpack, looked around the front room, and headed for the elevator. Gold upholstered chairs and ornate carved wood tables were arranged in small groups. A red carpet completed the traditional lobby atmosphere and there was a bar on the far end.

After a hot shower, Sally dressed in a clean shirt and slacks. She hand washed everything else in her backpack and hung clothes to dry on her portable clothesline from home. Her notebook, Kindle, and bathroom supplies went into the drawers of a bureau with carved dragons that matched the paintings on the walls. She sent a quick e-mail to Mary before taking a brief rest on the soft bed.

A CALL FROM THE HOTEL CLERK: HAN WAS DOWNSTAIRS. HE wore a white shirt open at his neck and blue jeans. He smiled and put his arms around her for a brief hug.

"Where are we going?" she asked, as they walked through the lobby.

"A restaurant with private rooms. I drive us." A dirt covered moped sat in front of the hotel.

Sally stared at the little green bike. "I'm going to ride on that? Look, there are big buses and trucks out there on the road." She pointed at the moped and then the street, in case he hadn't noticed.

"You not trust me? I have hurt feelings." Han sat on the green thing and grinned. He bounced on the seat and slid himself forward. "I make room for you."

Well, she said she wanted to live like a local. Just before climbing on behind him, she saw a Siamese cat near the glass doors to the hotel. The cat looked at her for a moment, then darted around the corner of the building.

Han called, "Hold on!" and seconds later they were roaring into city traffic.

Sally clinched her eyes shut. Wind blew in her face, the seat vibrated, she was surrounded by blaring horns, but she felt very alive. She snuggled close to Han and held him tight. His cotton shirt smelled like a man. It wasn't a black leather jacket, or the roar of a Harley Davidson motorcycle. But this was China and she was riding on a moped with a handsome Chinese man.

After daring to open her eyes, she began to enjoy his expert weaving around the cars and buses. When they arrived at a moped parking lot, she said, "That was kind of fun, Han. Except in America we wear helmets."

Riders on bicycles and mopeds did not wear helmets. Apparently, they were not viewed as a necessary safety measure. Sally decided that if anyone fell, they would be immediately flattened by a passing bus or truck. She had not seen police, fire, or ambulance vehicles.

"It good you like. I bring you to school on my moped every day."

Sally liked that idea.

They went inside a tall, narrow building. She followed Han up a set of stairs to a small room on the second floor with a round table and ten chairs. He led Sally to the back of the table across from the door. Frederick was by the door.

"You honored guest." Han explained. "Frederick sit by door. He pay bill."

Before Han could sit next to her, a pretty, young teacher took the seat, and flashed a friendly smile. Mei introduced herself. "I know Han many years. He can see you later. I teach Mandarin in Connecticut school for one year. I help you with food."

The other teachers introduced themselves and gave descriptions of their classes. There were two men in addition to Han and Frederick, and five women of different ages. Mei was on Sally's left. Juno, a vivacious woman, who appeared to be in her 50s, was on her right side.

Dinner was served buffet style on a lazy susan similar to the group dinner in Datong. Small dishes with vegetables, fish, pork and chicken pieces were on the turntable. The room was only large enough for the table and chairs. Once everyone was seated, the lazy susan could only be refreshed from the doorway.

Each person was given a small bowl of white rice with bits of ham, egg, onion, and spices to hold in their hands. Sally watched her neighbors hold the bowls close to their mouths and shovel the rice in with chopsticks.

Mei explained, "Yangzhou fried rice a regional specialty."

"Fried rice in America is dark, it's made with soy sauce," Sally said. "I like this recipe better."

"If you want, I show you how to make with sesame oil." Mei described many of the food choices for Sally.

All the teachers were eager to talk about America and what Sally could teach in her English class. Conversations were easy. Mei and Juno helped translate. Four teachers volunteered to guide her around school. Han said he wanted to be her Yangzhou guide. This was applauded by Frederick and several female teachers. Some of their comments made Han blush. He was seated on the other side of the table. Sally caught him looking at her and smiled.

Juno watched both Han and Sally. "You watch him, too." Sally blushed.

Two teachers used the English names they had adopted when they taught Mandarin in America. "A good idea!" Sally decided she would give her students a choice of American names to use during class.

After dinner Sally and Han went for a walk on the city sidewalk. She took his hand and said, "It was wonderful to see you at the train station. I was nervous to be here alone, I feel much better with you here. How long are you staying?"

"I have friends here. When I tell your success in my Shanghai class, they want you here. I make arrangement, take vacation. I can be with my friend. Would you like practice with QiGong Master? My Master in this city."

Sally's face lit up. She had not thought it possible to practice with a QiGong Master. "Yes! But I don't know QiGong. I'm a beginner."

"Everyone a beginner for my Master. I find when he available."

Han retrieved his moped with ease from the dozens of similar dirty bikes in the parking lot. They all looked the same to her. Different colors but the same dirt. And there were so many, all parked in tight rows.

During the ride back to the hotel, Han wove through traffic and pointed out the city highlights. Not only was she seeing Yangzhou, she discovered her fear of being in the middle of a street full of cars, buses, mopeds, and bicycles had reduced. She enjoyed the carnival atmosphere, the music of vehicle horns, and the play of colorful lights on store signs. Holding onto Han was a bonus. Exhaust fumes from nearby vehicles not so much, but it became part of the night's memory.

Back at her hotel room, Sally began planning her conversation lessons. To a list of boy's names of Bob, Mike, and John, she added famous American names, George Washington, Roy Rogers, Elvis Presley, Geronimo. The girl's names might include Betsy Ross, Marilyn Monroe, Elizabeth Taylor, and Annie Oakley. They could talk about what made these Americans famous. The name change would be fun.

MEI AND JUNO ARRIVED AT THE HOTEL SOON AFTER SALLY finished her buffet breakfast. She had said, last night at dinner, that she didn't have anything to wear to school and wanted something more feminine than cargo pants. The two teachers had quickly volunteered to take her shopping.

The clothing store was two blocks from her hotel. It shared space with an electronics store in a gray stone building. Bolts of colorful fabric were on the store shelves. Sally saw bright colored silks, cotton prints, and gray and brown fabric that looked like suit material. Womens' dresses and mens' suits hung on display hangers. The hum of sewing machines came from behind a curtain.

After a discussion with Mei, the shopkeeper, who had a head full of curls and granny glasses perched on the end of her nose, brought out a few skirts and blouses. All were too small for Sally.

"Looks like you need to have some clothes made for you. Let's look at fabrics." Mei was a "finder." She walked with a steadfast pace, knew where she was going and what she wanted.

"I've never had clothes made for me. Won't it take a long time?" Sally's eyes roamed around the store. This was foreign territory. There were shelves of thread, tortoiseshell buttons, and photos of smiling people modeling new clothes. She had trouble sewing on a button.

Mei shook her head. "No, only one or two days. Garments sewn quickly for foreign visitors."

The store manager pushed her glasses up on her nose and held up bolts of cloth to see what colors would look good on Sally. Mei and Juno shook their heads or nodded their approval.

They found two cotton prints for blouses and a dark blue cotton for a skirt. Measurements were taken. Sally admired the soft silk cloth on the display tables. A red silk with delicate white flowers caught her eye. She ran her fingers along the smooth material and pictured a dress for a special occasion.

Juno noted her dreamy look. "Why not have dress made from that? You can return to America with Cheongoam dress, like that one!" She pointed at a red sheath dress. "For special times." Juno's hair fell in short dark waves, her lips were painted pink, and she wore a flowered pink and yellow dress. She reminded Sally of a romantic Southern belle.

"It's so pretty. I would love a silk dress." Suddenly remembering, she asked, "Han told me he would bring me to the school on his moped. How am I going to do that with a skirt on?"

Juno answered, "You change at the school. Teachers come to school on mopeds or bicycles. We have lockers for our clothes."

More measurements were taken for a dress. The dress length was measured twice to be sure it would be long enough. An order was placed for two blouses, one skirt, and a special red silk dress.

After thanking the seamstress, Mei asked, "Do you need shoes? Your clothes will be ready tomorrow afternoon."

Sally held up her foot. "This is what I have for shoes. I only brought sneakers for walking." At a nearby store with mens' clothing, Sally bought slippers that fit her size 9 feet and would look good with a skirt.

MEI DECLARED IT WAS TIME FOR TEA AND DUMPLINGS, then led them to a small restaurant. Instead of a round lazy susan on the tables, each had space for four people. The aroma of cooked food came from a grill in the back presided over by two busy cooks. Steam escaped from round bamboo boxes.

Before entering, Sally glimpsed a Siamese cat that looked up at her and then darted behind the brick building. It looked like the one she'd seen at her hotel. And like Sasha.

She displayed her expertise on all things tea and dumplings and ordered her own by pointing to the menu. After the waitress left, she asked Juno and Mei, "Are there many stray cats in the city?"

"Restaurants sometimes keep cats to take care of the rodents. Dogs and cats are kept as pets, but usually inside," Mei answered.

Juno asked, "You're not afraid of eating cat, are you? We don't do that."

"Honest, I wasn't thinking of cat meals." Sally frowned. "I thought a cat outside looked at me. Maybe it was hungry."

"The restaurant will give it scraps. You're not going to feed it, are you?" Mei was concerned.

Sally shook her head. "I won't feed it. But it looks like my cat."

Juno sipped her glass of tea. "How do you know Han?"

Holding a dumpling with her chopsticks, Sally said, "I met him practicing Tai Chi in Peoples' Park in Shanghai. I was there with a girlfriend. My friend, Mary, came to China with her daughter and son-in-law. They adopted a baby girl. Han took us sightseeing. He's a very nice man."

"He likes you. Han a good man. We're happy see him smile. You get pretty dress, maybe special date in the future." Juno was clearly enjoying this conversation.

"Han is a good friend. I have fun with him. I'd like to go on a special date." Their conversation felt like girl-talk back home.

"Let's get foot massage. Do you have foot massage in America?" Mei came to her rescue, ending the romance conversation.

"We have massage and foot reflexology. I have friends who go to Chinatown in Boston for a massage. They say it's not the same on Cape Cod."

After walking down side streets teaming with people, they stopped at a store with a picture in the window of a woman receiving a massage. Sally was excited; she wouldn't have dared to venture this far from the hotel by herself.

Mei opened the door. They were greeted with smiles from a girl at the front desk. Sally thought she could have been a teenager, or in her late 30s. There was no way to tell. The three women were led upstairs to a large room with cloth-covered cots. Soft harp-like music, a bubbling water fountain on a table in the corner, and burning incense added to the tranquil atmosphere.

"Is that a harp I hear?" Sally asked.

Mei answered, "It is *guqin*. It has strings like harp, only seven. Very traditional. Girls study many years. They pluck strings with fingers and burn incense while playing. It's important to keep mind peaceful and concentrate to ward off evil spirits. Many people keep recordings for quiet time."

Sally changed behind a painted screen into a cotton wrap-around skirt and slippers, then she sat with Mei and Juno with her feet in a tub of warm lavender water. Marble-size stones were on the bottom of the tub.

"The stones are massaging my feet." Sally sighed with pleasure.

After they were done soaking, Mei instructed Sally to lie down on a cot. The masseuse, a young girl with a soft voice and dark shoulder length curls, handed her an eye mask. The girl began to rub her feet with warm oil.

The music, fragrant oil, and gentle massage put her to sleep. She woke with a start when the girl began slapping her feet and lower legs. The slapping continued until her legs tingled. "I never had a foot massage like this,"

"We will come again for facial and body massage. Massage important part of our culture," Mei replied.

Bouncing on her tingling feet, Sally asked, "How much do I owe?"

"Frederick gave us money from school's account. You not pay while you with us," Juno answered.

Sally was surprised. "Thank you! How do you say 'thank you' in Mandarin?"

"*Xiè xie*" Mei replied.

Sally turned and said *xiè xie* to the girl who had massaged her feet.

During their walk back to the hotel, Sally said, "The girl who massaged my feet had curls. Is curled hair popular?"

Juno answered, "Young women enjoy Western culture. Cut and curl hair. Color hair too. Our mothers cover gray hair with dye. I will bring you fashion magazine."

Sally smiled. "Juno, you are very fashionable."

At her hotel door she said good-bye to her new friends and peeked around the corner to look for the cat. The sidewalk was empty of cats

SALLY WALKED AROUND THE HOTEL NEIGHBORHOOD TO find someplace interesting for dinner. Vendors were selling steamed dumplings and green vegetables. She recognized bok choy. Meat was cooked on grills. The combined odors of the cooked food and various spices was so intriguing she decided on a street dinner instead of a restaurant.

Pointing at something that looked good and holding out her hand with coins worked wonders. Sally enjoyed a delicious dinner. When she saw a young woman at an ice cream stand, she pointed to a creamy orange flavor. The woman said, in English, "That is Mango Orange. Very good. It came today." She handed her the ice cream.

"*Xiè xie*. It is good." Sally enjoyed the sweet, slightly tart flavor.

A Siamese cat at the woman's feet looked up at Sally. "Hello, is your name Sasha?" She asked the cat.

After an answering *"meow,"* Sasha turned and walked toward the back of the ice cream vendor's stall. The cat stopped and looked up again.

"Okay, I know." Sally followed the cat behind a curtain into a room with a bed, table, chairs, and an electric wok on a shelf. The walls were covered with drawings of trees, flowers, boy and girl figures, and characters. The cheerful drawings looked like school lessons.

Sally smiled at a child sitting on a blanket over the floor, covered with blocks and plastic tops. The bright-eyed little girl reached out for Sasha.

Bending down, she said, "Hello, my name is Sally."

The ice cream woman came up behind her. "Her name is Cass and I am Nera, her mother. Our cat likes you."

"I have a cat like her at home, her name is Sasha. Does Cass go to school? I am here for a week to teach English."

Nera shook her head. "No, she not go to school. She is *heihaizi*."

"What is *heihaizi*? You speak excellent English."

"I was teacher. I am not married to Cass's father. When mother is not married, she can't get a *hukou* for child. Without a *hukou* for birth registration, child has no rights for education or medical care. I must go back to my ice cream stand now. Please come with me."

Sally looked at the little girl on the blanket and something tugged at her heart. "I'd like to talk with you about Cass. Would you let me come visit? I could talk to her in English." Nera appeared nervous. She kept looking at her daughter as Sasha paced between Cass and Sally.

"It is not allowed." Nera answered. "But it looks like Kitty Cat trusts you. Maybe you can come in morning."

"I'll come tomorrow morning at eleven and won't tell anyone."

Waving good-bye to Cass, she followed Nera out of the room.

When she returned to the hotel, she found the tables and chairs in front of the hotel bar were filled with men and women in suits and business-type dresses. A seat at the bar opened when a customer downed his drink and left. Sally quickly sat on a stool next to an auburn-haired woman.

"The hotel is hosting a convention of some sort. I don't understand Mandarin. Are you American?" She swiveled on her stool to face Sally.

"Yes, from Massachusetts. I'm here to teach English at the Yangzhou High School." She held out her hand. "My name is Sally Raymond."

"I'm Vicky Bradshaw from New York. I just finished a week teaching English and I'm leaving tomorrow to tour western China. I'm going to Tibet with two friends from home. We each started at different schools and plan to spend another two weeks traveling."

"Tibet! That sounds wonderful. I'd love to go there but I

don't think it's going to happen on this trip. What was it like to teach here?"

Vicky took a sip of her beer. "The students are very motivated. They start at 8 AM, then go home for lunch. Parents pick them up with bicycles and mopeds. Afternoon classes start at 2 and end at 5 for dinner. Students often return to school at 7 for study hall and tutoring."

"That's a really long day. Sounds like not much time for socializing." Sally was amazed at the dedication to education.

"Only about 30% of the students go on to college." Vicky continued. "There is a test given once a year, called a 'one shot test'. Education is very competitive, especially since the one child will be needed to support two parents in their old age. A married couple is responsible for four adults. A new government policy to allow a second child to each couple will change things in the future. But that will take time. They absorb everything you say like a sponge. It's a great experience. Have fun. Let them ask questions."

Sally found the idea of so much responsibility overwhelming. Her respect grew for the school's children.

THE NEXT MORNING HAN ARRIVED PROMPTLY AT 8. WITH A sweet roll from the breakfast buffet in one hand, Sally climbed on the back of his moped.

Leaving the city streets behind, they traveled alongside Shouxi Lake. Han pulled into a grassy yard with a small pool of large Koi and a flower-covered trellis. Lavender perfumed the air. An ancient man stood under the blue sky practicing Qigong.

While they watched, Sally paid attention to how he moved. He seemed to use a minuscule amount of energy, as if his body floated through space. He changed position so slowly she didn't detect movement.

Following Hans' lead, Sally bowed to his Master. She stood next to Han to begin Qigong practice with Master Quam. Concentrating, she tried to get her arms and legs to match his. As time went by, she became part of his circle, her strength increased, and she began to feel confident.

Master Quam stopped and motioned Sally to sit under the flower trellis beside him. He held her hands and began to chant in a melodic voice. She didn't need Han to translate, her body understood. She relaxed and allowed herself to meditate.

Much too soon, time with the Master ended. Sally whispered *xiè xie* and followed Han to his moped. The lavender scent followed her.

The bike would bring them to the crowded city with its exhaust fumes. The Master and Han had brought her into their lives while they practiced Qigong. She 'belonged' with them for a short while and liked it. Tired muscles felt rejuvenated. A feeling of well-being entered her.

She climbed behind Han on the moped, leaned forward, and whispered in his ear, "I'm strong!"

Han turned his head, laughed. "Yes, you are. I am happy I bring you."

"I need to go back to the hotel. I met someone last night who might be able to help me with my school lessons." She decided not to confuse Han with an explanation of a Siamese cat, Nera and Cass.

"I want to take you to Shouxi Park in afternoon. Very beauti-ful. I collect you at 2?"

"That sounds great."

She got off the moped in front of her hotel. Watched Han disappear into traffic, and walked to Nera's ice cream stand. The sidewalk was less crowded than last night. Nera was not outside, so Sally stood by the curtain and softly called to her. She could hear voices inside.

Nera pulled the curtain aside and motioned toward the chairs in front of her stand. "We can talk out here."

They sat down. "I read about invisible children in China before I came here," Sally began. "It is important for all Chinese people to speak English. I can teach Cass. Are there more chil-dren here? I heard voices." Sally knew she was talking too fast, but she was nervous. "Some children do not go to school. We have teaching here. There are books from older brothers and sisters who have school."

"Can I visit?"

Nera nodded, and led her to the room. Sally was introduced to two women and two children, between the ages of six and nine, sitting on a blanket. Carefully enunciating her words, Sally explained that she would speak English. Nera translated. Four sets of anxious eyes looked up at her.

Sally waited. Butterflies did somersaults in her stomach. She held her hands in front of her to keep them from shaking and began to wonder if she could do this. She was a stranger to them, and not sure about the legal issue of her teaching here. Would they be worried?

Suddenly, the women nodded and smiled.

She sat down on the floor blanket next to a young mother

and spoke slowly. "Hello, my name is Sally." Nera translated, and the woman replied with her name. The English lesson had begun.

As she walked back to her hotel, Sally thought about the consequences of what she had just done. She was a visitor in this country. It was her responsibility to be respectful of their laws. She may have just broken one. Tourist information had been specific about honoring China laws. Yet she had promised to return the next day. The mothers had accepted her, there was a bounce in her step. It felt good to have overcome her fear and to see the smiles on the faces of the mothers and children.

Later that afternoon, Han brought them to the city park. Foot paths meandered by ponds, over bridges, and up to pagodas. Weeping willow trees, soft grass, and artfully planted flower beds provided sweet air, a nice change from city exhaust fumes. Sally took deep breaths.

Han found a bench overlooking a pond. A small boy, holding a sailboat, ran to the water's edge. He set the boat in the water and clapped his hands as he watched it join a small boat fleet. The boy's mother talked to Han. "She say he wait all week for boat day. Park has boat-making kits. Children are proud of their boat and come to pond for boat day. His father help build boat."

"Tell her he is a handsome boy." Sally looked at the mother. "American children play with boats too. Is there swimming here?" Ducks gathered at the water's edge for offered food.

"Swimming inside, not here with fish and birds in water," Han crinkled his nose in dismay.

They walked over a bridge with five pagodas perched along

its span. Each pagoda had a different roof style, but all of them had curled eaves with protective figures on their tips.

Han explained, "Is called Lotus Bridge. During Qing Dynasty, Yangzhou very wealthy. Emperors built park with beautiful pagodas for tranquil time."

He held her hand and carried her camera. They stopped often for blond photos. Young couples were impressed to see an older mixed-race couple. The girls smiled at Sally and the boys stopped Han to ask questions.

Groups of school children followed teachers into the pagodas. Couples strolled holding hands. Fathers carried their small children. Older children walked next to their parents. There were no families with two or more children. When Sally held her camera up and pointed to a child, she received smiles and head bobs from the parents.

"Parents proud to have picture of child," Han explained.

"The young men carry the girls' handbags. Why?"

"It is custom. Always take care of girl. Not in America?"

"Women carry their own handbags. We shop alone, too. Men don't like to shop. In our culture the women like being independent."

"You want to carry your camera?" His smile gave away the teasing in his question.

"No. You look very handsome carrying my camera."

They visited some of the pagodas, and often stopped to smell and admire the colorful flowers. Sally took pictures of red roses, daisies, and yellow chrysanthemums. She managed to have Han in many of the photos. She wanted to remember this day when she was back home.

"I love it here. So many pagodas to visit. The white pagoda with the onion on top is my favorite."

"We can return." Han stopped walking and studied her face. His eyebrows formed a worry line. It looked like he wanted to say something, but instead took her hand to leave.

The moped roared. Under Sally's hands, Han's shoulders felt stiff.

She didn't want to say good-bye, and hesitated at her hotel door.

Han shuffled his feet. He looked away and then at her. "Frederick invite us for dinner. Aimee will teach you how to make Yangzhou rice. You like?"

Sally smiled. "Yes, I would, but I want to go to my room to change." And wash and put some makeup on, she thought.

Han definetely looked worried. Was it because she would be in their home?

When she returned to the lobby, Han was waiting by the front door. She made a quick stop at a street vendor to buy a bouquet of flowers for Aimee.

They left Yangzhou traffic behind and pulled into a cluster of apartment buildings. Han parked the moped in front of a row of storage units. Each space was locked with imposing padlocks on garage-size doors. A narrow yard between the condos and storage units was home to colorful bikes of all sizes, outdoor chairs and tables, and a swing-set for children. The metal doors on the condo tower were numbered.

"We go four floors up for Frederick and Aimee." Han took

the bouquet of flowers and started up the stairs. Paint was fading along the stairwell and wood signs on the doors were chipped.

"Han, slow down, please." She hesitated on the stairs, wanting to remember every moment of this special evening. This would be her first visit to a family's home.

At the door, Han told her, "They have mat for shoes inside and slippers for wear." He handed the flowers back to Sally and knocked.

Frederick opened the door, smiled, and held out his hand to Sally. Her tentative first step was awkward as she wasn't sure what to do about removing her shoes.

A young woman walked up to her. "Hello, my name is Aimee. Thank you for coming to my home." Her hair was cut in a short bob that gently moved with her confident stride. Subtle makeup enhanced her delicate features. She wore a yellow pantsuit with colorful embroidered flowers. She smiled warmly and showed Sally to a chair where she could take off her sneakers and put on soft red slippers.

Sally remembered she was holding flowers when she bent down to untie her shoelaces. "Thank you for inviting me. I brought flowers." Her hands were shaking. She hoped to make a good impression on Han's friends.

When she looked up after putting on the slippers, Han's eyes smiled, a message he was near. The same message he used during Tai Chi practice. Sally relaxed. There was no need to be nervous with Han at her side.

"Come with me, we find water for flowers." Aimee held the flowers and crossed the small living room, passing by a soft upholstered sofa and two chairs. Modern glass and chrome end tables held dragon ceramic lamps. A large photo in an ornate frame showed a young Aimee and Frederick in traditional red clothing. The striking photo was on a wall above a table with jade figurines.

"Our wedding picture," Aimee said when Sally stopped to admire the beautiful couple. "We have traditional wedding for family."

Sally smiled. "I see your home is a mix of modern and traditional. This is my first home visit here." She could see a bedroom off to her left, and a second room next to it with a row of windows that looked like an enclosed porch.

"I work in a Yangzhou store. We sell modern furniture for young people." Aimee's pride in her home was powerful as she waved to indicate the beautiful glass and chrome. "Frederick have family treasures, we show." She pointed to the jade figures.

The kitchen was small with a sink, hot plate, rice cooker, and shelves with dishes, cups, and glasses. Aimee found a glass vase for the flowers and in seconds had them artfully arranged. She set the vase on a small kitchen table. "We have dinner here."

Frederick and Han came to the doorway with glasses and a bottle. "Come join us for wine," Frederick invited.

They found seats in the living room and Frederick began talking. "Han stay here while in Yangzhou. He tell us you are pretty and smart, and tell him about America with big houses, and families with many children. Do you like China?" Frederick spoke in the same direct manner he had used while coming from the train station.

Sally sat on the sofa next to Han and felt him press close for a moment. Reassured, she answered. "Your cities have many more people than America and the traffic is frightening, but everyone has been kind and I like the food."

"Maybe not bones," Han added with a smile.

She stopped and looked at her audience. They were listening with smiles on their faces. "I am very happy Han is here. He helps me with your customs. I look forward to English classes in your school. The children in Han's school were so cheerful. The experience was addictive."

Aimee asked, "Would you like to cook Yangzhou rice?"

In the kitchen, Aimee pulled a sliding door shut to close off the living room. "So we can talk without men."

The rice was ready in a rice cooker. Aimee got out an electric wok. She moved around in the small space with familiar ease. "Frederick is friends with Han a long time. Han is lonely after wife die but he not find new woman. We are surprised when he call to tell about you. He said you are good teacher and he wanted to see you again."

She felt her heart jump. Han had been talking about her, and it apparently was good.

Aimee added egg, chopped vegetables, and sesame oil to the wok. The kitchen took on the aroma of a Chinese restaurant. "I see you are good couple. He is happy with you. You have happy face when you look at him."

Sally blushed.

Aimee added the rice to the wok mixture. After she put the lid on the wok and adjusted the temperature, she turned to Sally. "Han has something to tell you. Don't be afraid. He is good man."

Puzzled, Sally answered, "I know Han is a good man. He is

always kind to me." A sigh, "I like the way he looks. He is strong and graceful. His eyes are . . ."

A KNOCK ON THE DIVIDER STOPPED THE CONVERSATION.

"Is rice ready? We have dumplings." Frederick produced a bag with steamed dumplings.

Sally giggled. "Take-out in China? In America it is very popular to have Chinese food from restaurants delivered for dinner."

Dinner conversation centered on Yangzhou history and holiday traditions. To Sally's relief, the discussions were interesting, but impartial. She wasn't asked about her time with Han.

"I take Aimee to get us dessert," Frederick announced when the rice was all gone.

Sally looked at him. She was pretty sure he was holding something back. He had a tight-lipped grin on this face.

"Let's go." Aimee poked her husband in the ribs. Then looked at Han. "You will be good." She gave him a brief hug.

Frederick gave Han a thumbs up, then held the door for his wife.

Sally and Han were left standing in the middle of the living room. She felt goosebumps on her arms. "This is awkward. What's happening?"

"We sit on sofa, I have a conversation to tell." Han sat down and leaned back. She sat next to him. He didn't appear to be nervous. He turned to her and folded his hands in his lap.

I bet he rehearsed this, Sally thought. She kicked off her slippers, curling her legs under her. She was close enough to touch his hands. If he wasn't nervous, there was no reason for her to be.

"When I was fourteen China have bad time. Not enough food, many people starve. Chairman Mao told us it was rich people who are bad. He said peasant people must be strong. We didn't understand Communism. Children read *Little Red Book*. They have Red Guard in schools. They say rich must share. If not share, Red Guard came and burn furniture, burn books, arrest people." After a moment of silence, he added, "I was in Red Guard."

His face was solemn, sad.

"Did you hit anyone?" Sally remembered her dream in Datong. Had he been like that?

"No, I not hit people. I burn books, important papers, China history. I watch beatings, I not try to stop. I hear teachers crying, I not try to stop." He paused to shake off the memory. "I am punished. I do not have children. My wife is sick and die. I care for you. I not want to make you sick." He was trembling.

She wanted to touch him, say something comforting. This was a Han she didn't know, a man who had watched violence, who grieved a past with an intensity that frightened her.

Sally held her breath, her mind raced. He knows I live in America, yet he is afraid for me. She liked this man. A lot. Her life was about to become complicated.

"Your past can't hurt me, Han. I am healthy and strong. What you did in the Red Guard was a long time ago. I did things in the past I wish today I hadn't. I've had to forgive myself."

She was thinking about Michael but didn't want to talk

about him. This was Han's time. He needed to move on, away from his past.

Taking his hand, she stood up and brought him to her. His trembling ceased.

Holding on to him tight, she asked, "When do Frederick and Aimee come back?"

Han held up his cell phone. "I call when ready."

"Wait a few more minutes. I like this."

Sally looked into his dark eyes. She was sure he was more handsome now than when they had entered the apartment.

The ride back to Sally's hotel gave her an opportunity to hold him. His kiss goodnight lingered. She lay on her bed. It was hard to fall asleep.

EARLY THE NEXT MORNING, MEI ARRIVED TO TAKE SALLY TO pick up her new clothes. One skirt and two blouses made mix and match outfits. When paired with silk scarves, Sally would be fashionable in China, and later in Cape Cod. They were about to leave when the shop owner came running. She held the red silk dress in her arms.

"She wants you to try it on for a fit," Mei translated.

Sally tentatively touched the dress. It had cap sleeves, a Mandarin collar, white piping that matched the delicate white flowers in the print, and tortoise-shell butterfly buttons across the left shoulder. She slipped on the sheath. The soft silk slid over her body with ease. She enjoyed the smooth sensation as it covered her skin.

A discussion followed on how long the skirt should be and

how high the side slit should go. Sally stood in front of the mirror, entranced. She was returning home with a traditional Cheongoam dress, a treasure. Smiles from Mei and the store owner confirmed that the dress was gorgeous and sexy.

"I will have a party at home to show off my dress."

"Dress will be ready for a special date in Yangzhou," Mei suggested with a smile.

Sally felt her face flush. She wanted to wear this beautiful dress on a date, with Han.

After it was properly pinned, Sally rushed back to the hotel. Han was coming to fetch her soon. Her job at the school would begin after the student's lunch.

WHILE HAN PARKED THE MOPED IN THE TEACHER'S LOT, Sally watched the students running back and forth across a cement patio. Groups of girls and boys ran in relays.

"They run for exercise in morning before school and again in afternoon after lunch," Han explained.

"Everyone's smiling, and they talk with each other while they run. I'm not sure American kids would enjoy running in a line like that. They'd probably rather play a sport."

The students, dressed in school uniforms, moved with practiced precision. Bookbags bounced on their backs. All of the students ran. Nobody stood on the sidelines.

"They are in class all day. Need to be outside, exercise." Han was puzzled that Sally found this unusual.

Sally wondered about the health benefits of breathing the polluted city air. "I met a teacher from New York at my hotel who told me the students' schedule. It's a really long day."

The girls' dark hair waved back and forth across their shoulders as they ran. Dressed in identical uniforms, they all looked similar to Sally. She hoped she would recognize her students in class.

Han delivered her to the teachers' lounge. "Have a good day." His hand brushed her waist as he passed by.

Sally changed into her new skirt and blouse, and put her dusty pants in a locker for the return moped ride. The familiar school lockers reminded her of first-day-of-school jitters she had every year when she taught school. There were always new faces, new names. Sometimes last year's students would stop to say hello and ask about her vacation. She knew the school layout, she had her year's curriculum ready. Still, she'd been nervous.

This school was a challenge. Her heart raced, and she took a deep breath. Not only was the school unknown to her, she didn't understand the language the students and teachers were speaking to each other. She was going to be on her own in the classroom.

Frederick walked with her to the classroom. He stopped to point out a girls' restroom, the school library, music rooms, an auditorium. A paper sign on a classroom door read: "Welcome to our school" in large red print.

She felt a wave of doubt sweep over her outside the class as she waited for Frederick to open the door. In Shanghai, Han had been with her in the classroom. He had translated when the students spoke Mandarin. Today she had to take the full responsibility to teach English to the kids. English was her language. She didn't remember someone teaching it to her. It was always there. And she had taken her knowledge for granted. She put her hand on her stomach to quiet the butterflies and took a deep breath.

"Ready?" Frederick asked.

Sally nodded, then followed him into the classroom. Twenty, 10th grade students stared at her.

"Hello, my name is Sally Raymond." She wrote her name on the blackboard. "I live on Cape Cod in Massachusetts, in the United States." She walked up and down the narrow aisles between desks. Students followed her, turning their heads, sitting sideways to watch as she stopped to look directly at a girl or a boy.

The close confines of student desks allowed an odor of chalk dust and bodies to permeate the air. Sally could hear the students' breathing.

She held a handful of 3 x 5 cards. While she walked, she explained, "I have the names of famous Americans on these cards. We can use an American name in class. Raise your hand to choose a name."

One girl tentatively raised her hand. Sally held out a card. "Marilyn Monroe was a popular actress. She had blond hair, like mine, and blue eyes. Would you like to be Marilyn?" With a wide smile the girl took the card. Sally looked at her. "Hello, Marilyn. Your blond hair is beautiful today."

Lots of giggles. Eager hands began to wave. Spending a few minutes with each student so they could choose their name, Sally quickly relaxed.

Hearing murmurs in Chinese, she reminded them, "Only talk English in this class, please."

A boy raised his hand. "Do you speak Mandarin?"

"No, I do not. When I was in school the only foreign languages taught were German, French, and Spanish. People expected to travel to Europe, not Asia. Mandarin is taught in many schools in the United States now. I find the different tones used in Mandarin difficult to learn."

A girl's hand was waving. "Mandarin is like singing."

Sally laughed as she walked to the front of the room. "My singing is not good. I will sing if you will sing with me."

"You are my sunshine, my only sunshine, you make me happy when skies are gray." The students laughed. After she repeated it several times, the class joined in, emphasizing the high and low notes. Sally switched to *"Row, row, row your boat."*

The door opened a crack and a teacher peeked in. "Other classes are beginning to sing." Oh oh, was she in trouble on her first day? Sally changed direction. "Ask me a question." Hands went up.

At 5 o'clock Han was waiting in the teachers' lounge. Sally was relieved to hear, "Good job today!" from several teachers as she walked in.

After she changed into her street pants, she followed Han outside. With a twinkle in his eyes, he teased, "Would you like to hear some Chinese songs? I know a place with beer and lots of singing."

She laughed. "So, you heard."

"You are popular teacher, maybe not so much singer," he joked.

She bumped his side as they walked. "Are you suggesting a karaoke bar? What time?"

"I pick you up at seven. We eat first."

They joined the line of mopeds leaving the lot. Parents loaded children onto bikes. School books were slung on their backs.

Sally said goodbye to Han in front of the hotel. Nera's ice cream stand was her next stop.

"Hello, Nera." Sally was tired and in need of a sugar fix. "What is today's special flavor?" she asked.

Nera scooped out two mounds of a mint green ice cream. "Green bean ice cream. Very Chinese."

Sally wasn't sure about bean ice cream. Careful not to make a bad face to insult her new friend she took a small lick. "It is good! How do you make ice cream from beans? It's different and I can taste some mint."

Nera answered, "Make bean soup first. Also have red bean ice cream, see?" She pointed at a dark red mound next to the green bean ice cream. "Cass hope you come again."

"I would like to visit now, is it a good time?"

Still eating her ice cream, Sally followed Nera behind the curtain. Cass and a girl from the morning group sat on the floor playing with Hello Kitty dolls.

"Where's Sasha?" Sally asked.

"Kitty?" Nora shrugged, "She goes when the girls play with dolls. She is, how you say, jealous?"

"Yes, jealous is a good English word. My Sasha at home meows when I talk on the phone. She wants me to talk only to her."

"Kitty come to my ice cream one day. I feed her. Cass call her "Kitty", she say a good name." Nera bent down to talk to the girls.

The girls clapped their hands and moved over for Sally to sit with them.

"I thought I would talk about numbers in English."

"Good. I teach Chinese numbers." Nera pointed to some papers with characters.

"Do you know how to use fingers on one hand to show numbers one through ten?"

Sally looked at her hand and moved her fingers up and down. "No, I can only get to five with one hand."

"We teach you. Good for vendor who not hear, or not know English."

Nera held up her thumb: "one." Cass followed suit with her chubby thumb. Together they demonstrated two through five from one hand by adding fingers. Nera went on, "For six, little finger and thumb extended out, rest closed." Cass demonstrated with her tiny hand. "Seven is thumb and all finger tips touch, like make a beak. Eight is thumb and first finger make an L, other fingers closed. Nine is first finger make a hook, bend at knuckle, other fingers closed. Ten is all fingers closed, make a fist."

"Thank you, Cass, that is a good lesson." Sally wiggled her fingers and smiled at the girls.

Cass and her friend smiled and repeated the exercise.

They held out their hands to show how to bend fingers properly. Sally resisted the urge to give both girls a hug. They were adorable. She needed to ask Nera if a hug would be okay.

Sally told the girls the English numbers one through ten. She used her fingers, then their dolls and toy blocks to demonstrate addition. The girls repeated her words. She was amazed at how fast they learned the English words.

All too soon, Nera came behind the curtain. "Many people outside, hear voices. Must end for today." She turned to look out and then motioned Sally to follow.

The girls waved goodbye.

"Can I come in the morning?"

Nera smiled and nodded.

HAN WORE A BLUE TEE SHIRT WITH A CHINESE CHARACTER and jeans. He moved toward her when she got off the elevator. "You are very beautiful!" He took her hand and walked toward the door. "We meet Frederick and Aimee at bar for singing."

"Good! More singing." She touched his chest and asked, "What does this mean?"

"My school symbol. There will be teachers and expats tonight. I advertise my school." He smiled at her. "I sing for you."

BRIGHT LIGHTS AND LOUD MUSIC ADVERTISED THE BAR. Han parked the moped among its contemporaries in the bike parking lot. He led them down an alley to a small cafe, the front open to the street. Four tables with two chairs each sat along one wall. Two young men cooked in huge woks over open fire grills along the opposite wall. Sally smelled sesame oil.

She wrinkled her nose and said, "I don't see menus."

Han turned to look at the cooks. "They have chicken and noodles. Dinner special for today."

No longer afraid of chopsticks or bones, Sally tucked into her bowl of ramen noodles. Small family restaurants specialized in serving one meal a day. She had seen tables in front of living quarters in Shanghai. Sleeping space was probably in the back behind the curtain.

Han asked her questions about how the school here compared to America schools. She explained schools in America had much shorter classroom days. American children had homework after school. After she answered his questions, she asked, "Do all children go to school here?"

"Not all children can have school. Some learn at home."

"I see children on the streets during the day," she was thinking of Cass.

Han turned his head to look at an empty nearby table. "Some children can't go to school. Our government make one child only for families. When another baby come, cannot be registered." His hands twitched and face muscles tightened.

Sally said, "I know about the one child policy. People on Cape Cod have adopted girls from China."

Just then Frederick and Aimee appeared in the front. Aimee wore a silver lame pantsuit, high-heeled silver sandals, and large silver disk earrings. Her eyes twinkled and she held Sally in a warm embrace. "Are you ready to have fun?"

Han put his arm around Sally as they walked to the bar next door. Opportunity for conversation ended when they entered. Couples sat at tall tables. On a stage at one end a man held a mic and sang along with a record. It appeared to be a popular song as he was accompanied by many men from the audience.

Western young men and women mixed with Chinese at the

tables. Seeing her questioning look, Han leaned close to her ear. "Many expats live in this city."

Several couples broke loose from their tables and engulfed Frederick. "Hey teach! Join us."

Chairs were pushed around a table that held pitchers of beer and bowls of pretzels. The newcomers were introduced during a break in the songs.

Sally found herself next to a redheaded woman while Han visited neighboring tables and received handshakes, shoulder bumps, and shouts of joy.

The redhead introduced herself. "Hi, I'm Emily." Emily wore a tee shirt with a school symbol. Her British accent was familiar and reminded Sally of Alexandra. "Han is a popular teacher. Students and teachers come for his history lectures. I go when he visits Yangzhou."

When a new singer took the stage, their conversation ended.

Han's eyes were glittering when he found his way back to her. The emotional welcome from teachers and past students had brought a look of pride to his face. He moved his chair closer to her as he sat down.

Singers took turns on stage and chose songs in English or Mandarin from the karaoke machine. Frederick and Han were pulled to the stage for a duet. They were joined by shouts of joy and sing-along lyrics from their table.

Emily shouted in Sally's ear, "They sing naughty song!"

Han made a karaoke selection and began a slow song. He held out his hands to Sally.

"He sing love song. Go!" Emily gave her a shove.

Chairs were pushed back to make room for Sally to get to the stage. The crowd quieted and listened intently as Han took her hands. Sally's head was filled with music and the scent of friendship. She was part of his gang. She didn't need to understand the words of the song to know how he was feeling. Her heart was thumping a rhythm of absolute joy.

The hotel lobby was deserted when Han brought her inside. Their goodnight hug had been long and intimate. Sally crossed the lobby to the elevator, smiling, each step lighter as she welcomed the warmth of her breath. She felt young again ...

"You need to tell him."

Sally sat up in her bed and looked at the picture of Michael on her bureau. "I don't know how. He's been hurt, I don't want to hurt him more."

"Tell the truth. You are married. To me."

"Michael, I will love you always. If I tell him he may want to stop seeing me." Sally felt tears pool. She wanted to be with Han.

"He told you his past. He trusts you. Do you trust him?"

Sally lay back on the bed and pulled a pillow over her head. Michael was right. She had to tell Han. Even though Michael was in a coma, she was married.

Betsy Ross asked, "Do you always eat with fork?"

"Yes, unless we go to a Chinese restaurant for dinner. Then some people eat with chopsticks. Americans cut their food in small pieces on their dinner plate with a knife and pick up the bites with a fork. Chinese cut food into small pieces before cooking and use chopsticks to pick up the food."

George Washington asked, "Is it same food? Pictures show big bird on plate, white cream food, bread for dinner. No rice."

Sally smiled, "That sounds like our typical Thanksgiving dinner. American families celebrate holidays at home with traditional food. Thanksgiving is one time a year to celebrate the Pilgrims' arrival in America. Families cook a turkey, whole, then the father cuts off slices of meat for the family at the dining room table. They have mashed potatoes with gravy. Americans eat lots of potatoes. Potatoes are easy to grow in America." She had not anticipated this conversation line and wasn't sure where to go next. So she asked George, "Where did you see the picture?"

George answered, "There are picture books of America people. Our teachers from America say they go to hotel for special dinners."

"In America we see pictures of Chinese eating with chopsticks. Do you think pictures in books and magazines are like real life?" Sally wondered if cultural indoctrination extended to photographs. The class had taught her how easy it was for a meal to become a lesson in the world's differences.

Hands waved. Students were energized. Timid students now expressed their excitement in the class. Boys and girls were bouncing in their seats, eager to talk about their views on what they had seen and read in books. Sally enjoyed their inquiring minds and felt goosebumps on her arms.

George Washington said he saw cartoons. He wanted to understand why they were funny. Why did the artist draw people that looked mean or sad?

Girls liked the American fashion magazines. They wanted to know about makeup, and new styles popular in America.

Sally was surprised to learn that Chinese magazines liked to hire blond models. Expats' blond children were popular for little-girl fashion ads.

The class ended, and Sally thought about how she fit into their world. Books on etiquette in China were available. She was responsible, as an American representative, to be honest and careful when discussing cultural differences.

On her way to the teacher's lounge, Sally wondered if there were traditional rules for dating. She didn't know what they might be, and she didn't have a lot of time to learn. Her relationship with Han was advancing at breakneck speed. Last night's time in the Karaoke bar had definitely felt like a date. She didn't know what to do next, or, if she needed to do anything. After all, this was Han's country, maybe she should follow his lead.

Mei met Sally in the teacher's lounge. "Students enjoy talk about pictures. They see your country in pictures and like you to explain."

"I'm learning too. I had no idea how frustrating it would be to not understand cultural differences. The class is teaching me your habits and I teach them English words." Sally shuffled her feet and concentrated on how to ask Mei her next question. "Is what I am doing with Han the right way to date? I'm not sure how to act with him. It's getting harder, not easier."

Mei was quiet for a moment. She nodded her head as if making a decision, then said, "It's time we go get your red dress. You can go with Han on special date. We can plan. First a massage."

Later, when Han arrived to pick up Sally, she was waiting in the courtyard with Mei. Mei waved him away. "I take Sally today."

"This was an awesome idea." Sally followed Mei's lead, and

changed into a cotton wrap in the massage parlor; and was now lying on a cot. The lovely young girl who had given her a foot massage was now about to give her a full body massage. A cloth mask covered her eyes. The familiar lavender scent reached her nose.

Mei was on the cot next to her and asked, "Did you enjoy evening with Han?"

Sally moved her head to the side, toward Mei, "Han is a friend, but last night felt like a date. We were drinking beer, laughing, and singing with his friends."

Mei took off her mask, propped herself up on her elbow, and looked at Sally. "You don't know? Chinese men don't date. He courts you."

"But my home is in America, I live there." Sally sat up and took her mask off.

"In China men and women choose one partner." Mei stated. "When time together is good they commit. Married couples sometimes live separate. Jobs often in different cities. Han was good husband. There are teachers in my school with expat wives."

Sally struggled with her next words. "I have a commitment in America. I need to talk to Han. I wish there was more time." Her voice was wistful.

Mei exclaimed, with her customary take charge attitude. "I will make time for you to be with Han to talk." She then lay back down to allow her massage to continue.

Sally listened to the *guqin's* gentle music. The water fountain in the corner gurgled.

The massage left Sally's skin soft and pink. The red dress slid down her body. Mei and the dressmaker agreed it was ready, but not for wearing with her school slippers or sneakers. This dress needed special shoes.

Mei asked, "What size do you wear?"

"I have big feet, size 9. I don't think we can find heels here for me."

"We have American teachers here. I find shoes!" Mei was on a mission.

SALLY HAD THE EVENING TO HERSELF, HAN WAS DELIVERING his lecture in Mandarin. He had promised to give her a private history lecture in English.

A neighborhood noodle café provided dinner. Then, she spent an hour in Nera's back room with Cass and Sasha, laughing and playing hand games. After a beer at the hotel bar, she went up to her room to prepare notes for the next day's class on government. She was tired, traveling had changed her body's routine. The soft hotel bed took charge and she slept.

THE CLASSROOM'S ODOR OF CHALK DUST, AND THE SOUND of sweet voices struggling with English words made Sally smile. Time had traveled faster than she wanted it to. Morning lessons with Cass and her friends ended too quick. Yangzhou school lessons had formed a bond between her and the children. She thought, "I'm good at teaching English!"

She found Han chatting with Mei in the teacher's lounge while he waited for her to change clothes. His stride, as they walked to his moped, was crisp. He avoided eye contact, and conversation. After she took her place behind him on the moped, he turned and said, "Mei say you want important talk with me."

Sally stiffened. She reached to touch his chest for courage. "Yes. I need to talk to you. It's important. Can we go someplace private?"

"We can go to park or Frederick home." His mouth was a tight line.

"I felt comfortable in their condo. Can we go there? Please?"

He pulled his cell phone out of his jacket pocket. After a brief conversation, he put the phone back and started the moped.

Sally rested her head on his back. She wondered if this would be her last chance to hold him.

Their silent approach to the condo ended with Aimee's friendly greeting at the door. Sally took off her shoes and padded after Aimee in fuzzy pink slippers.

In the kitchen, Aimee arched her eyebrows, and in a cautious voice asked, "Do you tell Han goodbye?"

"No! But I have something to say about me. I'm afraid he will tell me goodbye."

"He is afraid. I tell him you not say goodbye. You will drink tea I make for you."

Aimee brought a tray with a white china teapot and two round teacups into the living room. Sally followed with paper napkins. Aimee placed the tray on a small glass table in front of the sofa and motioned her guests to sit. After a brief conversation with Han that finally brought a smile to his face, she left.

Sally reached for the teapot with a shaking hand.

Han's hand gently touched hers. He raised the teapot and poured two cups. Then, held one out to her. "Lavender tea."

The cup was warm in her hands, they had suddenly become cold. The tea was comforting, she sipped it.

"Go on. It's okay. You are safe." Michael urged her to talk.

She felt a surge of warmth emanating from Michael and turned to Han. "I lied to you." She sucked in her breath and, before he could say anything. "It's not exactly a lie. The lawyers say I might as well be a widow. My husband is in a coma."

"You have husband?" Han leaned back on the sofa, away from her. His face turned pale. "You are married?"

"Yes. There was a car accident five years ago. My husband almost died. He is in a coma He sleeps, and the doctors say he will never wake up. He's in a hospital. I visit him there. It hurts me to see him like that. I loved him so much. It took years for me to accept I am alone, but I have a new life now, on my own."

She stopped there. The room's silence stretched for an eternity.

Finally, he looked at her, "I don't understand. You can be with me when you have husband?"

Her tears flowed unchecked. She didn't know how to explain how they could be together even though Michael was alive. She took a deep breath and then said, "I can be with you."

He whipped her face with a napkin. "You want to say more? I want to stop talk now."

The moped ride back to the hotel was swift. The pounding of her heart was louder than Yangzhou's city wail. When she got off the bike, Han hugged her. His strong arms held her. He wasn't shaking. "I bring you to school tomorrow."

She railed at Michael in her room. "I could have

spent more time with him. I didn't have to tell him about you."
The dragon paintings mocked her. A reminder of how little she
knew about the country she was visiting. "I didn't think it would
hurt this much! You don't know everything Michael." She
allowed herself to grieve.

A spark of hope entered her thoughts after a night's sleep.
Maybe it wasn't over with Han.

HAN SMILED AT HER BEFORE TAKING HER HAND TO HELP
her board the moped. "You leave Yangzhou soon, would you like
another Qigong lesson with my Master?" His eyes were dark,
confident.

"Yes. I would like to practice with him again." She remembered how relaxed she had been in his Master's yard. What did
Han have in mind with this invitation?

Afternoon classes were a welcome relief from Sally's stressed
and confused thoughts. The children grounded her in the
present. School lessons were one day at a time for them. She
wished she could share their optimism of what lay ahead.

Han had made plans for them to visit his Master after her
classes ended for the day. His Master was waiting by the koi
pond in the fragrant garden. Again, Sally did not understand the
words he spoke to her, but she felt the sincerity in his voice. She
shared the Qigong exercises with Han. Afterwards, the master
motioned her to sit on the bench under the flower trellis. He
held her hands, bowed his head, and chanted in a
prayer-like voice.

Sally watched clouds move across the sky and listened intently. She wished she could understand.

Shadows had formed when the Master stood and walked towards his home, leaving Sally with Han.

"He say he will see you again." Han's eyes followed the distinguished man.

"I felt warm and loved when he sang. He is special. Thank you for bringing me here. I needed to relax." She wanted to say "after last night" but didn't, it looked like Han had something to say.

Han sat next to her on the bench, held her hand in his, and began. "I tell Frederick and Aimee you have husband. Frederick say American's have different culture. Your husband sleeps, you have alone life. He tell me I must understand. You are good woman. You tell me truth." Han squeezed her hand and stopped Sally from interrupting his speech. "Aimee say I am old fashioned, I respect traditions too much. She say you are right, you can see me." He moved toward her and said, "I want to see you more."

HER LAST MORNING WITH CASS AND HER FRIENDS HAD been both sad and joyful. Mothers had brought treats to share. Children presented Sally with colorful drawings. They smiled and laughed; and used English words. Nera's tearful hug almost unhinged Sally.

Nera said, "Thank you. Cass can speak English words. I hope you will come back to Yangzhou."

Children in her classroom had given her thank you letters

and sang to her. First in Mandarin and then in English. The song wished her a safe journey home.

A formal invitation, from Frederick, to teach for a year, was presented in the teacher's lounge. Teachers encouraged her to come back. The contract included an apartment and stipend pay.

THE DINNER DATE NIGHT HAD ARRIVED. MEI AND JUNO MET at Sally's hotel room to help her dress.

She had been allowed to shower in private, but it ended there. Mei handed her a silk camisole. Her legs would be bare under the dress. There was that revealing side-slit. Juno took charge of makeup. Sally was dusted with powder. Eye liner and shadow applied, and red lipstick that matched her dress. Nail polish highlighted her hands. Her blond curls were piled on top of her head with a shell comb. Then the dress and perfect silver sandals.

Almost finished, Mei gave Sally a small silk bag. "A gift from Han." Pearl earrings tumbled onto her open hand. As she hadn't been allowed to look in a mirror, Juno placed the luminescent pearls in her ears.

A full-length mirror reflected brown eyes made to look larger with dark eye shadow, pink cheeks, red lips, and curls crowning her head. A side slit in her dress reached above her knee. Juno stood next to her and demonstrated how to expose her leg to the best advantage.

A phone call from Frederick announced the men were downstairs.

Han wore a dark gray suit, white shirt, red tie and a wide grin. He extended his arm for her to hold; "Not ride my moped tonight." In the back seat of Frederick's car, he added, "You are beautiful. In Chinese we say *Měili*."

Quietly she answered. "*Xiè xie*, you are handsome. In English, *Wow!*"

"WE HAVE DINNER IN A GARDEN NEAR THE RIVER. "VERY romantic." Aimee explained from the front seat. "Frederick and I have table, not close."

Han led her along a garden path. "You have garden in America. When do you return?"

"I go to Xian from here for a week and then to Beijing. Mary is coming from America. An expat I met in Datong has planned day trips for us. I am sad to leave here. Yangzhou has welcomed me. I 'll miss you."

"You can come back. You can teach in school. I can be here."

Sally held back tears. "Will I see you again before I go home?"

Han hesitated, "After Beijing. There is a place, Guilin, in the south, a beautiful river."

Dinner included wine, Han explained "better than beer." His goodnight kiss was long. He whispered in her ear, "I remember from Shanghai "Be strong."

She buried her head in his chest. He smelled like wine, park dirt and flowers. She felt herself tremble with fear, sadness, and something more: Desire.

6

YANGZHOU

HAN

Han sat in the backseat of Frederick's car with Sally next to him. Frederick and Aimee were bringing Sally to the train station. She was leaving him today.

A week ago, he had felt such joy in this car on the way from the station to Yangzhou. She had been in the car, and he knew he would see her every day. Today he was sad. He wouldn't see her tomorrow, feel her arms around him on the moped, hear her laugh. The cute bubbly sounds she made in her throat were contagious. He always laughed with her.

Sally held the cell phone he had given her cradled in her hands. He'd programmed it so one button called him. His ring tone for her was wild bird songs. He wanted her to remember their walk in the park.

He also wanted to ask her to come back. If she taught school here they could travel to Tibet, Mongolia, rural China. They could go to his beginnings in the mountains, and the ocean beaches. Maybe she wouldn't miss Cape Cod.

Why didn't she say something?

Frederick spoke in Mandarin but his tone let everyone in the car know he was exasperated. "You got to tell her, man. She can't read your mind. What's the matter with you? You need to talk to her!"

Aimee sat next to her husband in the front seat. "She likes you. I think she wants to come back but is a little afraid." She turned around and gave him an informed stare. "Put your arm around her, hold her hand."

Han understood. He had to let her know how he felt. He bent forward to look into her eyes. "I want you to come back." He named all the places they could go together. "You can teach here. I can move to Yangzhou." He explained how the school had apartments for expats. They could practice Tai Chi together. "I can tell you China history. We can go to monasteries."

She lifted her head and smiled, squeezed his hand. He felt her melt into him. He wanted to cook for her, bring her to the park every day so she could have flowers.

"I will take care of you."

As soon as the words left his mouth he knew they were wrong. Her eyes opened wide and her body stiffened.

"Idiot!!" Frederick roared. No translation was needed.

Aimee shook her head. In a sweet voice, she scolded. "Sally is an independent American." In English, she told Sally, "You need to forgive him, he is man. Sometimes stupid."

Sally laughed. She put a finger to his lips to stop him from saying more. She leaned forward to kiss him.

"I have to go home. I have responsibilities." She put her head on his shoulder. "But before I go, I want to see the beautiful Li River in Guilin, with you."

Han smiled. It was not good-bye. He could make a plan for Guilin, then find a way to keep her in his life.

HAN WATCHED HER CLIMB ABOARD THE TRAIN. STANDING alone on the platform, he had one more thought. She has husband. He sleeps for five years. What if he wakes?

7

XIAN

SALLY

As her taxi drove alongside the Xian wall, Sally looked up at the rock fortress. This was where soldiers had stood guard centuries ago. The wall dated back to the Ming Dynasty. At 40 feet tall, 8.5 miles long, and 40 to 46 feet wide, it was the most complete city wall still standing in China.

Below the ancient ramparts, the modern city flowed from old to new and back to old again. Her taxi passed *hutong* neighborhoods with narrow streets full of vendors, and office buildings of glass and steel.

Sally gripped Han's cell phone, her only physical connection between the new adventure ahead and her emotional week in Yangzhou. She closed her eyes. So much had changed in her life, and there would be more. What was the future for her and Han?

The hostel was next to small shops and food vendors. She might have missed the door to the narrow building tucked among the neighborhood stores, but her taxi driver waved and pointed to a sign: "Hostel World." Her purple backpack slung over her shoulder, she opened the door and walked under a long string of world flags. In the lobby the pretty desk clerk smiled and said, "*Ni hāo.*"

Sally said, "Hello!" and handed over an envelope from the Yangzhou hotel. Inside was a hotel card and note in Mandarin. The girl called to a young man behind the bar, for a brief conversation. Both employees smiled at her. Were their smiles related to her blond curls or the message in the note? After the desk clerk gave her a room key and a towel, the young man from behind the bar introduced himself. "*Ni hāo*, I am Chao. I can take your backpack to room for you." He smiled, took hold of the backpack and headed for stairs in the back of the room.

Travelers of all ages filled the bar and lounge area. As Chao led her up four flights, he said, "Good up here, no noise from street."

Her room had one small window that overlooked the street, a single bed and two shelves. A shared bathroom was next door. After unpacking, Sally returned to the lobby where her fellow hostel inhabitants were gathered around long tables with bowls of pretzels and bottles of beer. Cushioned chairs and small tables were grouped to make space for private conversations.

Sally ordered a beer at the bar, then walked to study the tourist bulletin board. Daily trips to see the Terracotta Soldiers were advertised, along with bus tours to the city wall. She chose an all-day trip that included the Terracotta Warrior Museum, Imperial Tombs and Gardens, and a silk factory visit. The cashier at the front desk took her reservation for the next day's tour.

The bar area was popular. A group of college-age kids occupied two tables. Sally stood with her bowl of dinner noodles, looking around for an empty chair. A middle-aged woman waved, and called, "Over here!"

Happy to have company, she joined the woman and her two friends.

"Are you American?" The woman was slender, with cropped gray hair. When Sally nodded, she continued, "We're from France. I'm Anna Dubois. We've been in China a month, got here yesterday. Are you going to the terracotta museum?"

Sally nodded, "Yes, tomorrow, are you?" And sat next to a blond pixie dressed in green. The woman smiled and said, "I'm Portia Moreau. I can't wait to see the soldiers. I taught middle school before I retired, and Xian was on my wish list. What brought you to China?

Sally had a mouth-full of noodles, nodded, then answered, "I came with a friend. Her daughter and son-in-law adopted a little girl in Shanghai. I guess I'm an accidental tourist, I stayed on after they went home."

The third woman leaned over to say, "Welcome to our group! I'm Gloria Laurent." She twisted the yellow and green silk scarf around her neck. Jade earrings hung from her earlobes. "My daughter has a shop in Paris, and I'm her round-the-world buyer. The three of us have been traveling together since we retired three years ago."

"Did I hear you right?" Sally raised her eyebrows. "Have you all been traveling for three *years*?"

Anna laughed, "We're nomads. I was a travel agent, and I always wanted to see and do what I planned for other people. I learned a lot of money saving tips, like staying in hostels. Our families have their own lives now. We go home for holidays and when we arrive, laden with presents, they are always happy reunions."

The women continued to talk while Sally ate. When she finished her noodle bowl, she took it, with her empty beer bottle, to a side table for used dishes. When she returned to the nomads' table Chao brought her another beer. She didn't remember ordering one but smiled and said *xiè xie.*

She asked Anna, "Full time travel must be expensive! Even with the low hostel rates, you have to pay for plane and train transportation. My original plan was to be here for one week, but when I started learning about the history and seeing the art, I wanted to stay longer so I put my return plane ticket on hold. What did you do with your homes?"

"I've been a widow for a long time, so I downsized years ago." Anna said, "I gave up my three-room flat and stay with my daughter when I'm home. We work in the countries we visit. We get jobs teaching and stay with families. Free room and board are provided for private lessons. The families are great, they take us on day trips and teach us their language. I stayed with an terrific family in Beijing before coming here."

The idea of visiting other countries interested Sally. "Your English is perfect. Do you also teach French? How do you find the jobs?"

Gloria answered, "There are nomad blogs with information on good places to stay, alerts on bad experiences, lots of details. The idea is catching on. Women from all over are traveling." She looked at her friends, "What do you think? Is Sally a nomad-in-training?"

Everyone laughed, and Gloria added, "My daughter, son-in-law, and granddaughter live in my home. Stephanie's shop is successful, and I supplement my income by buying for her."

Sally asked Portia, "Why are you a nomad?"

Portia giggled. "When I was a teacher, I always had living quarters at the schools. I don't have a home. My son teaches at Oxford. I teach children during our travels now, and they teach me. I like being part of a group. We have fun together and take turns deciding on the next place to visit." She looked at Sally, and said with a shy smile, "I have a friend in Italy I visit."

"A male friend," Sally assumed.

"Let's get some rest," Anna suggested. "Our tour starts early and it's going to be a long day."

Sally followed her new friends upstairs. Their idea of traveling was interesting. They were friendly, and fun. She decided she'd ask them more questions about the nomad life on the bus to the Terracotta Museum.

A PHONE MESSAGE FROM HAN ASKED HER TO CALL. HER finger poised over the white button, Sally wondered if she could have a relationship with him, only visiting occasionally? Han wasn't comfortable with the fact she was married. And, to be honest, she wasn't sure either. Han had allowed himself to be vulnerable and told her he cared. She hadn't told him how she felt. Was she being honest?

Sally took a deep breath and pressed the button. "Hello, Han. It's good to hear your voice."

AFTER A BREAKFAST OF TEA AND DUMPLINGS, SALLY JOINED her new friends on the bus to the Terracotta Warrior Museum. She sat next to Portia, hoping to ask her about dating a man in another country. If she were at home, there would be lots of time to get to know each other before asking personal questions. She couldn't wait here, "Are you dating the friend in Italy?"

Portia nodded, "I met him on a tour in Florence. He has a vineyard and is busy with his grapes and wines. He travels to sell his wine. When we want, the three of us visit and stay at his villa. It works." Portia looked at Sally and smiled, "Why? Have you met a man?"

Sally felt herself blush. "Well, yes. In Shanghai. I feel strange about it. I didn't plan on meeting someone. But I like him. He came to Yangzhou to spend time with me."

Portia was grinning, "The guide wants our attention, but I want to hear more. Let's talk later."

The somber faced older man spoke English, "I am guide for today. My name is Zhang." He told the group a discovery story.

"In 1974, three farmers decided they needed a new well. Can you imagine their surprise when a shovel fell through into a deeper hole? After finding pieces of terracotta they began to dig more. They found a buried statue." He described how China had brought in archaeologists, historians, and carpenters to build three structures to protect the statues. "More have been left untouched underground. We leave them until we know how to protect them from outside elements. The statues were painted bright colors, but the paint disintegrates when exposed to the air. Without books to record history, the existence of the clay army had been forgotten. We wonder what else is buried. We know that Emperor Quin Shi Huang's grave is nearby and has been left untouched."

Sally was excited. The army in photographs was unbelievable, she would soon see it in real life.

Zhang added, "One of the original farmers may be in the gift shop to sign books."

The women exchanged adventure stories as the bus moved past the farmland outside Xian. The visitors from France had been to Japan. They said the cities were less populated, but much more expensive for travelers. They had spent time in Beijing and gave Sally a must-see list.

Anna said, "Be sure to visit the Olympic Village and the *hutongs*. Tienanmen Square is good for Tai Chi. Eat ice cream. Shop in the underground malls. Be sure to use the bathroom in upscale clothing stores."

This brought side-holding laughter, but all three shook their heads and refused to tell Sally what was so important about the bathrooms.

THE BUS PULLED IN FRONT OF A LONG BUILDING. THE group was instructed to first watch a film about the hidden army. Sally stood in the theater-in-the-round and watched army battles. The film told the story of a monarch's desire to be protected in death. There were scenes that showed how the artists created clay soldiers and horses.

The science and artistry in the film could not prepare the visitors for the magic behind the museum walls. Humbled by the incredible army of terracotta soldiers and horses, Sally was reminded of the power in China's past. The silence shared by the throngs of visitors a sign of universal respect.

She joined the tour, stood above the army, and looked down at an emperor's dream.

ZHANG WATCHED THE MEN WORKING BELOW FOR SEVERAL minutes, then said, "There are 80,000 soldiers in formation, waiting for orders. Life-size horses stand ready to pull a chariot or seat an officer." After a pause to allow tourists time to digest the scene, he continued, "Many have missing heads. Bodies were cast from similar molds, but the heads were made individually. The archaeologists have proven this as the ears on each soldier are unique. Ears are like fingerprints, distinctive to each person."

Sally didn't know that and reached up to rub her own, special ears.

"They were buried under a wood and sod roof. As time and weather disintegrated the ceiling, earth covered the army. China lost its history and people forgot."

Sally looked down at the men in white work clothes among the clay soldiers. They were digging, dusting, discovering, and preserving.

Zhang continued, "Come back in 50 years, there will be more."

After reading the information plaques, and viewing intact soldiers in glass cases, Sally wandered back to the catwalk above the clay army. The air seemed to vibrate with strength and serenity. It was easy for her to be drawn into an image of an ancient reality. A story began to take place in her mind. Her eyes closed.

A voice in her head formed an image.

"Dust filled the air. Wood burned in the ovens used to set the clay images. Incomplete statues were ready for heads. Artists painted bright colors on uniforms. Solemn clay soldiers stood ready to be placed in formation. Voices cried out in pain".

A nudge from Gloria brought Sally out of her trance. "The tour is leaving now for the tombs and the park." She smiled, "Were you daydreaming?"

Sally took a last look at the soldiers, and then followed Gloria to the bus.

THE SWEET SMELL OF FLOWERS, GRASS, AND TREES BLEW through the Imperial Park. Sally walked with the nomads past stone statues of military guardsmen in elaborate uniforms that seemed too cumbersome for fighting. Large stone elephants, lions, mastodons, and mythical horses with horns formed a sentinel line. The Emperor's final resting place lay beneath a grass-covered hill.

Gloria said, "I read how scientists have proven the existence of mercury gas in the burial chamber. Rumors are that it also contains buried treasures and terracotta statues of performers to entertain the Emperor in his afterlife."

Sally climbed onto a ferocious lion to have her photo taken. Above her head, brightly colored flags featuring China's history fluttered in the breeze.

Birds began to sing . . . in her pocket.

She pulled out her cellphone. "Hello, Han. I'm in a beautiful park sitting on a lion."

He laughed, "Is lion happy you are there?"

"I don't know, he doesn't understand English." She slid off

the lion and retrieved her camera from a smiling teenager. "I read in some travel blogs that the cost to go to Xian to see the soldiers was enormous and not worth the trip. They were wrong! The soldiers are a once-in-a-lifetime memory. How's school?"

"The children ask for report of where you are today. The blond lady's adventures are happy lessons for them."

Sally imagined him smiling, his eyes sparkling. His voice was seductive and raised goose bumps on her arms. "Tell them I say hello. Our guide is signaling, I've got to go. Can we talk tonight?"

"Yes, want to hear more. I would be happy to be in park with you."

After Han hung up, she added, "I wish you were here, too," then pressed the end call button.

Portia nudged Sally on the bus as it left the Imperial Garden. "You promised to tell me about the man in Shanghai. Now's a good time."

Sally looked at her new friend and answered, "I just finished talking to him. He calls me every day. I'm not used to that much attention from a man."

Portia smiled, "Do you like it?"

"Yes," Sally blushed. "When we met I didn't plan on a romance. But, after spending time with him in Yangzhou I feel different. I've been offered a year-long teaching job there and Han said he could be there, too. I'm tempted to say *yes*, but I have responsibilities at home." She didn't mention that one of her responsibilities was her husband, in a coma.

"I met Anthony during a tour in Florence. Italian men move fast. He invited me to his villa. We have a good relationship. He travels a lot but when we're together it's very romantic." Portia stopped talking about herself. "You have a great opportunity to try out the nomad life with a personal guide. I say, go for it!" She squeezed Sally's hand and looked out the window, "It looks like we've come to the silk factory.

THE BUS CAME TO A STOP IN FRONT OF A WOOD BUILDING adjacent to a gentle flowing stream. Zhang said, "You have tour of silk making here, and very good gift shop to buy silk." Then he ushered everyone off the bus.

Young girls sat in front of water troughs filled with mulberry leaves. Live silk worm cocoons rested in the water. With patience and dexterity, the girls pulled almost-invisible fibers from the cocoons. Six or seven fibers were then held together to form a thread and attached to a weaving machine behind the water troughs. They chatted as they worked. Harp music played in the background. An aroma of wet foliage filled the air.

"Silk became a China treasure after Empress Leizie found a worm in her tea cup," Zhang explained. "According to Confucius this was in the 27th Century BCE. The 14-year-old Empress began to unravel the floating threads. She felt the soft silk, and later wove them together into a strong cloth."

He led the group past the water troughs. "Silk has been found in remains of the Roman Empire and Egyptian tombs. Cleopatra liked silk. Xian is first city for Silk Road. The silk trade lasted more than 1,600 years. During Han Dynasty silk was used as currency."

The group moved toward the gift shop. "Silk worm farms were closely guarded. Selling or buying silk worms was illegal and punished by death. The precious worms were cared for by families for generations. After delicate threads were unraveled, cocoon shells became food for farmers. They could be ground up. The shells were also used for ladies skin care."

A map on the gift shop wall outlined the famous Silk Road from Xian to Rome. "Buyers came on camels to buy silk and transport it more than 4,000 miles overland." Zhang raised his eyebrows with a doubtful look, "It is said two monks smuggled the eggs in their hollow bamboo staves to Egypt. The worms grew and reproduced. And that was the end of China's silk monopoly."

Silk rugs, hats, and bags were for sale in the gift shop. Sally admired a kimono embroidered with a golden dragon. If only she could afford to bring home that treasure! Instead, she bought eight scarves for future gifts. They wouldn't take up too much backpack space.

As their bus drew close to Xian, Gloria said to Sally, "We're going on a discover-somewhere bus trip tomorrow. Want to come?"

"A discover what trip? Where are you going?" Sally asked.

Gloria laughed, "We don't know. We go down to the bus station and pick a bus. Ride it to the end, or if we see an interesting stop, get off. It's fun to ride with locals and visit the small villages. It's always a great adventure. We sometimes buy the local crafts. I've found some stunning embroidery at very reasonable prices for my daughter's shop."

"We did it all over Europe," Portia added. "And in Beijing and Shanghai. There are some great, small villages in China. The local food is amazing, and sometimes scary when we have no idea what we're eating."

Sally smiled, "I'm up for an adventure. Sure. I'll come."

When they returned to the hostel, Sally went to her room and found a card on the floor just inside the door. She picked it up, turned it over, and read about an acrobat show. It looked like a free ticket. The hostel didn't clean rooms for guests and she had the only key. The card must have been slipped under the door. But by whom? And why?

She set it on a shelf with her backpack and turned on her Kindle. There should be news from home. She read Mary's e-mail and answered with descriptions of the buried Army, an Emperor's legacy, and a teenage Empress's discovery of silk. "You can have a silk dress made in Bejing. They're very fast at sewing garments here," she told her friend.

Han sent an e-mail with notes from his students wishing her a "happy trip."

The Kindle was a connection with home. Peaceful silence surrounded her, and she took time to reflect on the day's discoveries. It was so much more than she had expected.

"DO YOU REMEMBER ROME?"

"Yes, Michael. I remember the coliseum, the frescos, the mosaics, the pizza, and red wine."

Sally had stood at the top of the coliseum with her husband. Together, they had imagined Gladiators and Roman history unfolding at their feet. They had marveled at the gorgeous church mosaics and walked the lovely piazzas. She had gotten tipsy on red wine. Michael held her hand and stared into her eyes.

Today she had looked down at rows of Chinese warriors, an Emperor's dream. She had marveled at silk masterpieces. The day had been a history lesson. Han had been in her thoughts.

Sally woke with a start. She sat up and rubbed her eyes. Two men were vying for her heart. "What now, Michael?"

"He can be with you, I can't."

She took out her camera and looked at her pictures of the terracotta soldiers. She backtracked to pictures of Han in a Yangzhou garden. Time had made a difference. The world had moved on to a new present. People remembered their history. The sorrow, pain, and loss, but they made room for a new future.

SALLY AND THE NOMADS ATE BREAKFAST FROM STREET vendors. Children ran to take their orders. The scene reminded her of Yangzhou and the invisible children. She missed their laughter and sweet sing-song voices.

Anna declared, "We better get our bus tickets. The buses leave soon."

The street crowd swelled as they approached the bus station.

Portia exclaimed, "It's my turn to pick." She walked up to the ticket window with an "English" sign and returned with four bus tickets.

On board the battered, dirty bus, the four women sat in their assigned seats near the back. Chinese women quickly filled the bus seats, most held cloth bags filled with boxes and paper-wrapped parcels.

Sally turned to Portia, "It looks like they've been to the city to shop. But why would they return in the morning?"

Portia looked around at the women and shrugged, "I don't know. I can ask later, after everyone settles in their seat."

"How?"

"I have an electronic translator,"

The bus engine roared and the driver pulled into the busy street. Sally looked out the window at the bicycles and asked, "By the way, where are we going?"

"I asked for a pretty city," Portia answered. "I can't pronounce the name." She held up a cell-phone-size gadget. "This is my electronic language dictionary. It's set to translate French and Mandarin, like language dictionary books do. I can say a word or phrase in French and it will repeat it in Mandarin." She demonstrated with "I want a toilet" in French. The device answered in clear Mandarin. It apparently worked well. Neighboring travelers turned their heads and frowned. Sally and Portia shook their heads and looked apologetic and tried not to laugh.

Gloria got out her device. "I'll ask my neighbor why everyone is carrying packages."

The two had a conversation, translated via modern technology. The translator's popularity grew and the women sitting nearby began a show and tell. They pulled out boxes and bags: toilet paper and soap, beans and cooking oil, pints of alcohol, and bags of tobacco were the most common items. Palm-size plastic-wrapped packages were described as "treats." Passengers laughed and exchanged opinions on their purchases.

"Women are the same all over the world. We love to show off what we bought." Portia commented after translating the French conversation for Sally.

Anna was sitting with two young women in the back of the bus. She used her translator. "They are bringing goods to their families in rural villages. Mothers and daughters work nights in Xian to support the families they leave at home. They bring supplies home during the day."

Fractured families, living in a society where separation was the norm, was a new experience for Sally. She expected to see the women show depression and sadness. But the passengers were all smiling, talking, and sharing information on the contents of their shopping bags.

The bus was loud and bumpy. It made clanging noises, jerked back and forth with transmission changes, and the horn sounded before each street crossing. Stop signs and traffic lights didn't exist. The city suburbs were quickly replaced by apartment complexes with gardens, goats and donkeys. Farm animal odors wafted into the bus's open windows. Country homes often were sprawling cement dwellings for two or more families.

Portia smiled and pointed out each change in the landscape.

"Do you ever get tired of the constant travel?" Sally asked. "I'm really curious about the nomad life."

"It was a challenge in the beginning. Getting used to the food is sometimes hard. My stomach doesn't like hot spices. I bring plenty of antacids. We've been to doctors on our trips, and even a hospital in Thailand when Anna fell and broke her ankle. Our translators have been a godsend. If you plan on traveling more you'll need a translator."

"I have one! Han gave me a cell phone in Yangzhou to call him any time." Sally held up her phone to show Portia.

Two hours later, the bus pulled into a village surrounded by a wall. As they passed through an archway, barely large enough for the bus, passengers began to gather up their belongings and call out to each other.

Gloria yelled over the din, "We've been invited to a restaurant for lunch. Follow the lady with the yellow scarf!"

The foursome followed their lunch hostess down city streets, past vendors with push carts, small eateries, and food spread on blankets. Progress slowed as Sally and Portia stopped to pose for blond photos.

During a particularly long session involving multiple poses with various family members, Sally asked, "Does an invitation to a meal happen often?"

Portia nodded, "Foreigners are celebrities. But we don't always eat, and we always stay on main streets. We got lost once in *hutang* alleys in Shanghai."

The yellow scarf woman stopped in front of a café with three small tables. She pushed two together, then greeted a smiling man and little girl who came out from behind a cloth curtain covering a doorway to the back. Sally looked around and raised an eyebrow. She told Anna, "I bet this is their home, and this is a family restaurant."

Anna nodded. "It looks like we're having a buffet. They're making room for lots of dishes. Do you want to stay?"

Everyone nodded *yes*. It was close to lunch time and they were hungry.

Birds sang in Sally's pocket. "Excuse me, it's my English-Chinese translator." She pushed the white button. "Hello, Han. Your timing is perfect. I'm in a small village with my French friends."

She shrugged her shoulders when he asked where. "I don't know. It took two hours to get here from Xian. A woman from the bus is making us some food for lunch. I don't know what. Would you please find out what we're going to eat?" She handed the phone to their hostess. After a brief conversation, she gave the phone back to Sally and went behind the curtain.

"She have good food, cooked vegetables, chicken, rice. Don't eat red peppers, very spicy. You have a good day, I call you tonight."

After Sally pushed the "end" button she smiled and said to her friends, "That was Han. I told you about him last night."

To Gloria's delight, vendors came into the café to display their jewelry, painted silk scarves, and a variety of jade and quartz ornaments. Price bargaining appeared to be expected. She bought several bronze bracelets, and a set of turtles that nestled into one piece. "I'll send these to my daughter. Her shop carries handmade jewelry."

With Gloria's encouragement, Sally negotiated a fair price for a silk square with a hand-embroidered yin/yang symbol.

Anna reminded the group, "We need to get our return tickets before they are sold out." She turned to Sally. "In Shanghai, we took a bus into the country and didn't get return tickets. When we got to the bus station to go back, the trip was sold out. It was the last bus of the day! We were lucky to find a hotel for the night. The hotel clerk called the hostel to hold our luggage."

After lunch, they each said *xiè xie* to the hostess and her family. And held out their hands with coins to pay the bill.

THE BUS STATION WAS NEAR THE VILLAGE WALL, AND AFTER purchasing their return tickets they walked toward a line of rickshaw drivers. The nomads conversed in French. They shook heads and waved their hands, then started toward the bicycle drivers.

Sally yelled after them, "What's happening?"

Gloria turned around and said, "Sorry, we didn't mean to be rude. We enjoy rickshaw rides. Come on, I'll negotiate." She led Sally over to a young man standing next to a black bicycle that was attached to a white two-wheel carriage.

Portia whispered to Sally, "She makes the best deals. There are four of us, so we can use two carriages. I get squeezed in the middle when we are three." She held her hand up for a high-five with Sally.

A second rickshaw was engaged by Gloria, and both drivers hopped on their bicycles. After all four women were seated in the rickshaws they pulled into the street. The strong legs of the drivers pumped the bikes with ease. A clanging bell announced their approach to side streets. Both drivers peddled alongside the village wall and stayed on narrow streets without cars or buses. Sally loved it. They traveled over a bridge into a park with green trees, a pond, manicured grass and colorful flowers. The drivers pulled to a stop in front of a pagoda. They waved at the women to go up the stairs.

Sally hesitated, "I don't want to leave the rickshaw. What if they leave while we're inside?"

"They won't. We haven't paid yet," Portia answered. "Come on, this must be a special place for the village. Let's go see."

Inside the tall, narrow pagoda, a golden Buddha sat on an altar. Candles shed soft light on embroidered cushions. A gentle breeze from open windows caused scattered wind chimes to sing. An aroma of spices came from small bowls of oil.

Without saying a word, all four travelers knelt on the cushions to pay respect to the tranquil Buddha. They knelt together, their shoulders touching. Sally whispered a prayer asking for guidance on her dilemma with Han.

The rickshaws were waiting where they left them. The women climbed back on, and the tour continued out of the park and into the streets, busy with all the sights, sounds, and smells of rural China.

Portia asked Sally, "The man in Shanghai, is it serious?"

"I don't know. He's courting me, says he cares, but I have a commitment back home." Sally's hands began to shake. "How does it work for you?"

Portia smiled, "I am content seeing him 3 or 4 times a year, but Italy isn't too far from France. Occasional visits from America to China would be a different story." She pointed to a group of children playing in an alley. "You could teach school for a while and get to know him better. We're never too old for romance."

On the bus trip back to Xian, Sally sat next to an old woman, who kept smiling and pointing at her head. She leaned over so her curious neighbor could touch her blond curls.

When they returned to the hostel, Sally overheard a conversation in the lobby that a group was getting ready to board a bus for dinner and an acrobat show in an hour. She remembered her free ticket and went to her room to drop off her day's purchases, wash her face, and change her clothes.

When she returned to the lobby the nomads were there. "I found this ticket in my room. Do they give free tickets to all the guests? Yours looks different."

Portia answered, "We bought ours yesterday. You better ask about yours."

Chao was checking tickets. Sally asked him, "Is this ticket good for tonight? I found it in my room."

He smiled and nodded. And ushered her onto the bus.

At the dinner theater, the hostelers were seated at various tables. She wondered why Chao seemed to be watching her, he was young enough to be her son.

After sweet and sour pork and a coconut-flavored drink, the acrobatic show began. Girls folded themselves into seemingly impossible contortions. Boys juggled plates and did handstands on stacked chairs. They performed mock Kung Fu battles using Tai Chi swords with three-foot blades.

During intermission, Sally asked Chao about a walking tour of the city wall. He replied, "Long walk. Bicycle good. I have friend. Maybe she can go with you."

"I need time to rest. How about the day after tomorrow? A bike ride sounds good, I need the exercise."

Back at the hostel, Anna commented, "The bartender pays special attention to you."

Portia giggled. "Maybe he has a crush on you."

"One man in China is enough for me." Sally laughed. "Besides he's just a kid." Sally shrugged, but she wondered why Chao was being extra attentive.

SALLY FOUND HER FRIENDS READING E-MAILS FROM AROUND the world the next morning. Anna had told her about women traveling alone or in small groups who shared information. There were nomads everywhere.

She was looking at the bulletin board when Chao joined her and asked if she enjoyed the acrobat show. He smiled and pointed at a Xian city map, "Muslim quarter good for dinner. Very beautiful. Good food, plenty shopping."

Hui Minjie, or Muslim Street, was Xian's Muslim neighborhood, home to approximately 20,000 people. The area dated back a thousand years. The Great Mosque was from the Tang Dynasty, and the gardens were open to the public.

Sally asked Portia if she thought her group were up for a trip to the Muslim quarter later that day. After a quick discussion they agreed on a time they would meet up at the hostel.

It was decided to take a cab. Split four ways, the fare was less than one dollar each. When they reached *Hui Minjie* Sally was surprised at the savory aroma of grilled meat. Food stalls were everywhere, lamb and beef kebabs were cooking on small stoves. "I haven't seen this much meat anywhere else in China," she remarked.

"We went to the Muslim quarter in Beijing. I loved the food there," Gloria said. She was looking for the perfect lamb kebab.

Anna reminded everyone, "Leave room for dessert. They make the best date dumplings and fruit pies. Really good."

Portia trailed behind. She waved at the fruit displayed on table tops, and said, "There are so many different kinds of dates for sale. Look: fresh, dried, different colors. And the nuts. Wow!"

They passed men with small white hats and white beards. Women wore colorful *hijab's* wrapped around their heads. Mosques were plentiful, a reminder that the Muslim culture continued in this village within a city. Sally found a stand selling silk *hijabs*. She purchased yellow, white, and red scarves for family gifts. The vendor demonstrated how to wind one around her head and shoulders.

Long tables were piled with mahjong games, paper lanterns, brass monkeys and turtles, and ivory and jade jewelry. But no Buddhas.

Sounds, smells and colors enveloped Sally in a haze of excitement. The festival atmosphere captured her attention. During an exchange of cameras so everyone would have photos, Anna explained, "We follow the Silk Road from here. Tomorrow we start."

"You're leaving?" Sally was startled. "You've only been here a few days."

"The train tour leaves once a week. And our jobs in Beijing kept us there longer than we expected."

"I'll miss you. You have been fun." Sally enjoyed her new friends.

Gloria linked arms with Sally. "We'll be back. The shopping opportunities here are endless. I'm sure my daughter will want more."

"If you decide to teach here we can get together again." Portia grinned, "I think you will want to be with your man."

The already crowded streets and alleys expanded in volume as dusk settled. The market took on the atmosphere of a bazaar. No one wanted to be first to say, "I'm tired."

Finally, Gloria reminded the group, "If we want to take a taxi back, we better go now. They will soon be too busy to easily get a ride."

THE WOMEN SAID GOODBYE TO SALLY IN THE LOBBY OF THE hostel early the next morning. Gloria said, "Our next stops are Turpan, Dunhuang, and Urumqi. We're on a train for most of the Silk Road. We teach school for a week in Dunhuang. I want to spend a night in a *yurt* someplace in the desert. Our plans aren't firm though, they never are. We're definitely going home for the holidays."

"Do you ever get homesick?" Sally asked. "I can't imagine spending Thanksgiving and Christmas away from home."

"I did, but not so much now." Gloria answered. "There's always someplace else I want to see. Our families are grown, they don't need us anymore. I go back, and everyone is excited to see me. Then, when my family returns to their normal routine, I plan a trip with Anna and Portia."

Portia hugged Sally, "The offer to teach in Yangzhou sounds great. It would give you the opportunity to see a lot more of China. There is so much more here than the regular tourist stops." She smiled, "And it sounds like you have a handsome, willing guide. Lucky you!"

Sally's eyes filled with tears. She was saying goodbye to her friends. They were walking out the door when she heard Han's cellphone in her pocket.

She looked at her watch. He was calling her before his first class. She felt her heart flutter when she thought about his smile. He would be smiling now. Han was a friend in China who was not going to leave her. She planned to leave him in a few weeks. To go home. Would she return to teach in Yangzhou? She asked herself that question before answering Han's call. She wanted to feel his arms around her. Her husband was in America. Michael was in a coma. It was unlikely he would ever put his arms around her again.

CHAO WAVED, "MY FRIEND HERE, SHE WILL TAKE YOU FOR bike ride on wall."

A pretty girl with eye-liner outlining her dark eyes and dressed in jeans and tee shirt smiled at Sally. "Hello, my name is Diane." When Sally looked startled, she added, "I am university student. I enjoy using English name."

"*Ni hǎo*, I am Sally."

After reassuring Diane she had ridden a moped in Yangzhou, Sally followed her out of the hostel, and climbed aboard the waiting bike. Then held on to Diane's waist for the familiar weaving in-and-out of traffic ride to an entrance to Xian's wall.

Diane parked her moped, took Sally's hand to cross the street, and said, "This is South Gate, very beautiful."

The steep staircase had a ramp alongside the steps. As they walked up the steps, several teenage boys ran by them going up the ramp. They ran down, then up again. They were showing off, and this time it wasn't Sally's blond curls that had garnered their attention.

Diane looked straight ahead. Her lips curled up just a bit. She told Sally, "Ramp built for horse to pull wagons up to top."

"Looks like it's for an athletic competition today." Sally smiled at her blushing guide.

At the top of the steps, a group of rickety old bicycles were available for rental. The male admirers from the ramp quickly sorted through the bikes. They presented Sally and Diane with fairly new bikes. The bicycles were smaller than adult bikes at home, with wide tires for riding on stone blocks.

Diane translated for Sally. "They plan to join us riding. I tell them to leave." She placed her backpack in her bike's basket. Then moved toward the boys with her hands out front, making a chasing motion.

Sally laughed, "I haven't been on a bike in years. I may be slow and need to rest. Let them stay. I would like their company."

After a slow start with some wobbling, Sally got her balance. With the boys close behind, they began the wall tour. The roadway on top of the wall was wide, as it had been made for horses and wagons. People strolled among the trees and flowers growing from large pots. Small children ran, playing a game, while older adults sat on benches.

Built in a time of turbulence for the purpose of defense, the wall now served as a peaceful refuge for the city's population. The wall had been completed during the Ming Dynasty when warfare was rampant. China's villages and cities built protective walls from dirt, and later, bricks and rocks.

Four young Chinese men in army uniform walked past. They held cameras and smiled at children. Sally thought about how their counterparts once might have lived and died here. The ancient spirits seemed to be alive in the air, Sally could feel their tears and pain.

The four gates were: *Changle,* which meant eternal joy, in the east; *Anding,* harmony peace, in the west; *Yongning,* eternal peace, in the south; and *Anyuan,* forever harmony, in the north. The park above the city was a beautiful tribute to Xian's history.

Diane made frequent bike stops to stand by the waist-high

rampart. She pointed out new buildings and old temples in the city below. "This edge made for soldiers to not fall off." She shared water bottles from her backpack with Sally. Each time they stopped, the athletic teenagers joined them to talk with Diane.

Sally began to feel tired. "I want to rest. It is difficult for me to catch my breath." Her throat hurt and her legs began to ache.

"We can stop, if you want. Go back." Diane began to wave the boys away.

"I want to see more. Just go slow. Keep your admirers with us. I enjoy watching their courting technique."

Diane blushed again, "They need important things to do."

"They have an important job now, escorting us." She pointed to a tall tower in the center of the city. "Is that the Bell Tower? I read about that."

"Yes, the Bell Tower. It has four stories. Once was fortress for defense, today museum. Very beautiful flowers, trees, and grass. At night, many lanterns make more beauty. You should visit."

Later, Diane pointed to a block of apartments around a playground. "Those are for people who come to work here from other countries."

"Do they work in your schools?"

"Yes. Hotel jobs, schools, and businesses."

Diane leaned over the wall, to point far away, "The Muslim quarter there. Many shops, good food. Xian beginning of Silk Road."

Sally nodded, "I had dinner there yesterday. I learned about the Silk Road and ate barbecue and dates."

The eight-mile ride worked leg muscles Sally hadn't used since leaving home. They had been riding bikes for three hours.

The young men took their bikes to the rental station. Sally said *xiè xie* to them and took their picture with Diane.

The staircase they took to go down was on the other side of the South Gate. Diane said, "We are in good *hutang* neighborhood. Many food venders. Do you want to eat?"

Sally was hungry. "Yes. Would you order something for me? Not spicy."

Diane brought a vegetable barbecue and tea. They sat on chairs to eat and watched the crowd in front of them. She was quiet. Her dark eyes looked into the distance. Finally, she asked in a low voice. "You teach school in America?"

"I don't teach school anymore. Why do you ask?" Sally asked. This seemed to be an odd question when they hadn't been talking about education.

Diane ushered Sally into an alley and pulled a phone from her backpack. She pushed some buttons and handed it to Sally.

The screen lit up. Nera and Cass smiled and waved.

"What?" After almost dropping the phone, Sally held it out in front of her. "Nera, Cass, hello! What a surprise!"

She turned to Diane. "How did you know?"

Nera answered for her. "Chao is my brother. I tell him you come, take care of you. Do you enjoy Xian?"

Sally laughed. She would e-mail the nomads about this revelation. They thought he had a crush on her.

"Your brother is very good to me. A very nice young man. Cass, I am lonesome for you. Say hello to your friends from 'Teacher,' please."

Sally wanted to stay on the phone forever, but after a few minutes of sharing her news she said goodbye.

Nera and Cass waved goodbye. Cass held up a squirming

Siamese cat. She waved Sasha's paw. "We say goodbye." Sasha said *"meow"*, and looked like she was ready to jump out of Cass's hands.

Sally turned to Diane. "Are there unregistered children here?"

Diane nodded, "I take you there."

They walked down two blocks. Diane led Sally behind a store selling electronics. She knocked on the back door. A young woman opened it, and after a brief conversation with Diane, she smiled and said *"ni hǎo"* to Sally. They were led to a room with five small children sitting on boxes of cameras, phones and electric rice cookers.

Sally looked at their upturned faces and knelt on a rug next to a girl with large dark eyes. *"Ni hǎo,* my name is Sally." She had done this before.

Diane introduced the mothers. "Their children cannot go to school. We teach. It is important they learn English. All China will speak English in future. It is, how do you say, for all countries?"

"An international language," Sally stated with a smile.

After playing games with the children for an hour they returned to the hostel. Sally asked, "How can I get to the children from the hostel?"

"They will bring you."

SALLY ORDERED A BEER FROM THE BARTENDER. "I KNOW who you are!"

Chao brought her a bottle and opened one for himself. "Nera and I from outside Xian. Farmers allowed two children if first is girl. Nera my older sister. I am birth registered."

He explained what it was like for Nera to live a secret life. "She work and take care Cass. She teach Cass. Someday Cass have job with English speaking. Nera's man want her to give away Cass. He not want to marry. She say 'no' and she keep baby." Chao looked sad when he ended his story. He added, "My sister is brave."

Sally listened and remembered her time with Nera and Cass and the other mothers and children in Yangzhou. She nodded, "Cass is happy. She is always smiling. Your sister is very brave."

MOPEDS CAME FOR SALLY. THE DAYS WENT BY FAST.

When Sally wasn't teaching, she rested. Her muscles hurt, her throat was sore. Then her chest began to feel tight with a deep breath. The polluted air was beginning to take its toll on her health. She spent hours in her room. Chao brought her tea.

HAN CALLED EVERY NIGHT. SHE WAS CAREFUL TO NOT mention she wasn't feeling well.

Chao was with her when Han called on her last night in Xian. When she ended the call, he asked, "Why you not tell him you sick? He your man, he take care of you."

"He lives in Shanghai. I just met him a few weeks ago. He's a friend. I live in America." Then Sally decided she could take a chance and tell Chao about Han's past. "You are too young to remember the Cultural Revolution, when children were in the Red Guard. Han was in the Red Guard. He feels sorry for some of the things he did. He thinks he is responsible if I get sick. I don't want to worry him."

"I know about bad times in history." Chao answered. "University have books." Then he took Sally's hand and said, "He old Chinese, have respect. He call you. He wants to be your man. Do you want him?"

Sally looked at the phone in her hand and smiled. "You make it sound simple."

Chao hugged her. "In China it is simple. You can be with him."

BEIJING

SALLY

The flight from Xian to Beijing took two hours. Outside the terminal the air was heavy with smog and smelled dirty. Sally found a young man with a taxi by the open door. He grinned and nodded when she gave him a card with the name and street of a hostel.

She was anxious to see Mary, there was so much to tell her friend. Three weeks in China seemed like a lifetime when she thought about the news she had to share. But she had a headache. Holding her backpack by one strap, she dragged herself into the hostel lobby.

Mary jumped up from a seat facing the door and ran to give Sally a warm hug. "Wow, it's good to see you. I calculated how long it would take you to get here from the airport and I've been drinking beer for over an hour. You look really tired! Your eyes have red lines."

"I am! My eyes hurt. And it smells bad here." Her smile was

weak. She coughed. In a strained voice she added, "Beijing is the capital city of China. The Emperors lived here. Why is the air so foul? It's just not right."

"It's smog." Mary shook her head. "There was smog in Shanghai too. Beijing has become an industrial city." She led Sally further into the entrance. "I checked us in but you need to sign in with your passport."

After Sally settled in their hostel room, she joined Mary at the bar. "I don't understand. The Chinese are smart. They should be able to figure out something to get rid of this smog. It's not healthy!" She grabbed her beer.

"I think they're working on it. The one child only per family policy was to reduce population growth. I read they're replacing coal and wood burning stoves in the *hutangs*. So, tell me about Han. What's happening with him?"

Sally sipped her beer and began to feel more relaxed. "It's a long story."

"We've got all day. Well, half a day, it's noon already. I scheduled a tour of the Forbidden City for us tomorrow morning. The bulletin board here has some interesting tours. So, tell me, she said with a smile."

"He met me in Yangzhou."

Two beers and an order of french fries later Sally finished her story. "We're going on a Li River cruise after I leave Beijing."

"Is he coming here?"

"We didn't plan on it, but Han is spontaneous. It wouldn't surprise me. Now, tell me about Hope. What's it like to be a grandma?"

"I thought you'd never ask. She's perfect. I have pictures.

And look, Sasha is with her. Collen brought her to their home to care for her and your cat won't leave Hope's side."

Sally looked at the photos of a little girl and a Siamese cat. "I've found Siamese cats during my travels here that remind me of Sasha. She looks happy."

"She is," Mary answered; "You may have a difficult time convincing Sasha to move back with you when you get home."

After more pictures and descriptions of what Hope had learned to say and do in America, Mary asked, "Do you feel like a walk to Tienanmen Square?"

Sally stood up and stretched. "Sure. Sitting on the plane and now here, my bottom is sore. A walk sounds good."

Mary took out a notebook, "The city park is a must see. I made notes at home. It's 100 acres of numbered cement slabs. The numbers allow people to meet and parades to assemble easily. A smart idea."

"Come on! I'll show you how to cross the street." Sally stood with Mary on the street corner across from the park. When a group of young people began to cross the street she quickly grabbed Mary's hand and crossed with them. "I learned how to cross streets without getting run over. I cross with the locals."

Tourist groups wearing identifying tee shirts or holding matching umbrellas followed their guides. They listened on earphones to audio presentations. Foreign families and visiting nationals sat on benches, eating vendor food and taking pictures.

A family wearing colorful woven jackets were sitting on a blanket. They reminded Sally of pictures from Mongolia, with dark complexions and small eyes. The guide in Datong had pointed out to the tour group how tribal physical differences in China were due to the varied climate and geography. She had pointed out her eyes were narrow, and her nose had a round ridge. It made it easier for her to see and breathe in the windy mountains.

Mary pointed to her camera and received smiles and nods. She took photos of a child with mom, dad and maybe an aunt and uncle. Sally thought how interesting it would be to visit Mongolia, where the people lived a nomad life close to nature. She wanted to ride one of their horses.

Young soldiers in crisp uniforms walking in pairs passed by, casually talking but alert, with roving eyes. The communist presence was made known.

A photo of Chairman Mao and his granite memorial was a popular photo stop. Sally thought about Han's boyhood time in the Red Guard. Han was still tortured because of his past. She wondered if the young people who honored Mao today, by visiting his body in the granite tomb, knew all the details of the China Revolution. America didn't teach about the government's brutal treatment of the American Indians. What was the responsibility of teachers; didn't students deserve the truth about the past?

Groups practiced Tai Chi in the square, children with teachers, men doing kicks, women moving with gentle serenity. Sally wondered if they would let her join them. She missed practicing with Han.

Children flew kites. Beautiful birds and dragons waved in the sky.

It felt good to be with her friend again. She hadn't smelled salt air or walked a beach in weeks. She imagined the taste of a bowl of New England clam chowder. Was she homesick?

"It looks like everyone in this park is from somewhere else. They're visiting and then they will go home."

"That's what you do when you go on vacation," Mary replied.

"I've been so busy. I forgot all this is temporary." Sally waved her arms to encompass the entire square. "They say home is where the heart is. Why is home so far from here?"

As if on cue, birds sang her pocket. As she pressed the button to say hello, she looked at the tourists and realized that she, too, was a tourist.

"How was your trip?" Han's voice was a welcome addition to her day.

"The plane was full. They served us a nice meal. In America, all you get is pretzels and coffee or soft drinks. China flights are a luxury!"

Mary leaned in and hollered, "Hello, Han!"

Sally handed the phone to her.

Mary smiled, nodded her head, and answered his questions. When she returned the phone to Sally, she said, "He asked about Hope and my trip from America. He said he was sorry he was not here to take us on tours." She smiled. "He's a keeper. He remembered my granddaughter. I like him!"

Sally smiled, "I like him too."

Han was still on the phone. "It's hard to breathe here. The air is heavy." She didn't feel well and kept the conversation brief.

With the cellphone back in Sally's pocket, they returned to the hostel, and checked the bulletin board for trip ideas. She planned to visit with Alexandra after they got back from the Forbidden City. Alexandra had promised an afternoon of shopping and eating.

"Let's have Peking duck for dinner. I saw a recommendation for a restaurant near us." Mary was excited to try her find.

The dinner lasted almost two hours. Sally described how confused she felt. China was beautiful and mysterious. The people were friendly, but there was so much brutality and war in their past. She loved teaching the children, and she could do it for the next year if she wanted. She had a contract she could sign. And, there was Han. She had feelings for him.

Sally was glad to get back to the hostel. She was tired and lay down on the bed. Her eyes closed.

"Come home. I need you."

She pictured Michael in his hospital bed.

Tears welled-up in her eyes. She was an American. Her husband was in America. She was a tourist in China, like the visitors she had seen at Tiananmen Square. A sore throat mixed in with her tears. How could she feel so happy and so sad in one day? And so sick. She was pretty sure she had a virus.

BREAKFAST WAS ALMOST IDENTICAL TO THE ONES SHE ATE AT hostels in Shanghai and Xian. Sally drank hot tea and ate dumplings. She told Mary, "I've become addicted to dumplings."

Mary had her notebook out. She was studying her notes on the Forbidden City. "I got the *Last Emperor* movie from the library last week. It's hard to believe that the story and palace are real."

Sally answered, "After what I saw in Datong and Xian, I can believe the Chinese were capable of anything. Remember, they had lots of people, millions, to use for laborers. And they were very superstitious. Still are. All the dragons and mythical stat-uettes on roof eves are to protect against evil spirits. Their Emperor was a god."

As they walked across Tiananmen Square with their Forbidden City tour group, they passed people practicing Tai Chi. It was 8 AM and there were thousands of people beginning the new day with Tai Chi.

Their guide gave a brief lecture at the entrance to the first gate of the Forbidden City.

"You walk through three gates, have massive red doors and brass buttons. Rub the buttons for good fortune. The year 2020 is 6,000 year anniversary of Imperial Palace. It is considered biggest palace in world. It is on 180 acres, has 980 buildings, and was home to 20 Emperors from Ming Dynasty in 1368-1644 to Qing Dynasty in 1644-1911. The only male allowed in the inner court was Emperor. All others were eunuchs. Eunuchs were laborers, guards, and household staff. They held respected governing positions. When the Empire fell, many valuable jewels and historical icons were stolen by the eunuchs."

They walked through the Gate of Supreme Harmony into a courtyard guarded by giant bronze lions. The first palace, the Hall of Supreme Harmony had walls and tile roofs painted red for prosperity. The Imperial family's shade of yellow was used for decorations.

Sally was stunned. The palace was huge with intricate archi-tecture. Thousands of visitors surrounded her. Nothing she had seen, so far, compared to the quiet strength in front of her. She felt the spirits of the past embrace her.

Side buildings housed museums for gems and ceramic figurines thousands of years old. Glass cases allowed an up-close view. The art lured Sally into a mystery. How had they done such incredible carvings and paintings?

Dragons were everywhere, embroidered on the Imperial robes, painted on ceilings, carved into wood walls. A 300-ton granite slab with carved dragons formed a ramp along the stairs to the Hall of Supreme Harmony. Emperors were carried on sedan chairs over this amazing work of art by *eunuchs* walking on the side stairs. Sally walked up the stairs with the tourists and admired the delicate carvings on this immense rock. Earlier in the tour the guide had said it was brought to the Forbidden City between 1407 and 1420 in the coldest part of winter. It was dragged on a sled about 45 miles over a road made from ice. Workers had dug wells along the route to maintain a smooth ice flow for the granite.

An Empress and *concubines* had lived behind the palace and were attended to by *eunuchs*. "The *concubines* have small huts compared to the rest of all this," Mary said with a scowl. "Poor things. They could fall in love with a *eunuch*, maybe, but never, you know, whatever. The last emperor had a very sad life according to the movie."

Sally said, "There was an empress in China. The Empress Dowager Cixi ruled for 47 years. She had been a *concubine* that gave birth to the Emperor's only son. She was 25 when the Emperor dyed and she took over."

"Women's lib in China. I like it!" Mary made a fist and pumped the air.

They admired the emperor's chair within the third courtyard. Sally said, "I asked about *eunuchs* in Yangzhou. There were thousands in the Forbidden City." She pointed to a painting of *eunuchs* in elaborate robes. "Han told me families castrated their young son's so they could live in the palace with food and comfort. He said they kept the boys' genitals, pickled, in a jug. They believed if the jug was buried with them, the boys would be whole again."

Mary grimaced, "I find it hard to wrap my head around parents mutilating their son. I also can't fathom mothers binding their daughter's feet so she could make a desirable marriage. "All this splendor for one person seems unreal. But after seeing the terracotta army in Xian that was made for one emperor, I get it." Sally agreed.

A line of taxis outside the Gate of Divine Might stood ready to transport the dazed crowds away from the Forbidden City. Sally checked her watch. It was time to meet Alexandra for lunch.

ALEXANDRA WAS DRINKING TEA IN THE BEIJING International Hotel dining room. When Sally waved from the dining room entrance, Alexandra's face lit up. She waved to Sally and her friend to join her. "It's good to see you both," she said, and hugged Sally, then Mary.

Mary smiled at Alexandra. "Sally told me about your trip to Datong. It sounded like you two had a great time.

"We did," Alexandra nodded. "I was lucky to meet Sally. She talked a lot about you."

After they were seated at Alexandra's table, Sally asked, "Do you think I can get a cheeseburger here? That sign says it's an international café." She looked at diners eating what looked like hamburgers, macaroni and cheese, and lettuce and tomato salads.

"Sure!" Alexandra smiled. "They sell delicious cake and pie

for dessert, too. We can get to the underground mall from the hotel reception area." She raised her hand to get menus from a roving waiter. "I have an art class in mind for you two. And, an expat recommended guide for a trip to the Great Wall."

"I want to buy a dress for the embassy dinner," Mary said. "European fashions are not plentiful on Cape Cod."

Sally added, "I want to find a drug store. I need cough drops." She was exhausted after a long morning of walking. A cheeseburger and fries for lunch, soon gave her strength for an afternoon of shopping.

Alexandra led the women to the elevator to descend to the first of five levels of underground shopping.

THE THOROUGHFARE WAS BUSY WITH LOCAL AND FOREIGN shoppers. There were clothing stores for men, women, and children. Bright lights advertised shoe stores, furniture stores, and fast food shops. Neon signs advertised DQ, Kentucky Fried Chicken, and Starbucks. Food odors mingled with dust from the floor. Many people wore paper masks across their nose. The walkways were narrow, and more crammed than shopping malls back home.

An I-Phone trade-in stand caught Sally's attention. It had a slot to drop your phone in and push a button for a new phone. She watched a young man send an old phone out and retrieve a new one. It reminded her of how advanced China was with their electronic gadgets.

Alexandra led them to a drug store with its front-end open to the mall corridor. Mary wondered off to check out make-up and skin care selections. The sales ladies seemed anxious to explain to her, the wonder of their products.

Men and women in white jackets were talking to customers with health complaints at a counter with packaged goods.

Sally told Alexandra, "Don't tell Mary, but I'm really not feeling well. It feels like the flu. If she tells Han, he'll get upset. She talks to him whenever he calls me. I don't want to worry him."

"Sounds like the visitor flu," Alexandra answered. "It's from the change in food, change in air, all the rushing around, and new germs. We've got lots of strange germs here, that's why you see so many people wearing paper masks. To protect them from the germs and smog. It's common for visitors to get sick." Alexandra described Sally's symptoms, in Mandarin, to a young man behind the counter. He nodded and asked several questions, then gave Sally two packages.

Alexandra translated, "You have cough drops and a tea for your sore throat. They'll give you an English instruction sheet at the checkout."

They were ready to leave the store when Mary joined them, holding a small shopping bag. "Come look! There are bugs, worms, and dried weird things in the cases in the corner over there."

Alexandra said in low voice, "That's the prescription department. Tonics are made from the stuff on the shelves. I go to the hospital for my drugs."

Back out on the mall Alexandra steered them toward an elevator going to the lower levels. "This is where you'll find your dress, Mary. The higher quality clothing stores are on the lower levels."

"I remember, I'm supposed to use a Ladies Room here," Sally told her friends. "The nomads from France instructed me, with lots of giggles, to use a bathroom in a Beijing mall. They wouldn't tell me why." Sally wasn't interested in fashions.

The store fronts on the lower floor had changed. Loud music and glitter was replaced with subdued glamour. The hallway had fewer people. And the floor was clean.

Alexandra grinned and pointed toward a restroom. "In there. The first booth in line has a western toilet. I'll wait outside."

Sally walked into the stall and looked at the wall next to the toilet. Alexandra was standing in the mall waving at her.

"What?"

Sally laughed and waved back to Alexandra. She knew Alexandra couldn't see her, it was a one-way mirror, but, still, it felt weird to pull her pants down while strangers were wandering past right in front of her.

When Mary took her turn, Sally joined Alexandra in waving at a blank wall.

"Seems to be a big hit," Alexandra commented. "Chinese have an interesting sense of humor."

Mary found the perfect dress, and sweater, and belt. "Okay, that maxed out my credit card," she said with a grin.

"Good, because I'm really tired. I want to go back to the hostel," Sally answered.

SALLY ARRIVED AT TIANANMEN SQUARE AT 7:30 AM dressed in Tai Chi pants she had bought in a men's clothing store in Yangzhou. A sore throat was not going to keep her from practicing Tai Chi at the famous landmark.

A group of five women, who looked about her age, were stretching. She walked up and said, "*Ni hāo*. Can I join you?"

Everyone smiled and answered in Chinese. She didn't know what to do next. How could she explain what she wanted? So she did two Tai Chi poses. The women nodded, and gave her a thumbs up. Sally had been accepted.

She was placed in the middle of the group and they began morning exercises. They moved their arms and hands in graceful circles. A graceful flow that began at the shoulder and ended with the tips of their fingers. It looked like a rippling river. Sally matched her legs and feet to theirs. Each move showed strength and confidence. At the end of the practice, the women surrounded Sally. They pointed at her clothes and talked to each other.

"You've improved. Looking good!" Mary had come to watch.

"I wish I knew what they were saying. They're really interested in what I'm wearing." Sally pulled up her shirt sleeve to show skin underneath. The women pulled up pant legs and sleeves to show her what looked like long underwear.

A young man joined the group. In English, he said, "It's customary to wear more clothes beginning September. Hello, I am Li Cheng. They say you are good Tai Chi, have pretty yellow hair. Are you American? They ask how old are you."

"*Ni hāo*, I am Sally Raymond. Yes, my friend and I are from America. And I am 55, how old are they?".

After he asked several questions of the women, he answered, "They are ages 70 to 80."

Mary was startled. "I better start doing Tai Chi I want to

look like them when I'm 70. Hello, Li, I'm Mary Callahan. I just got here yesterday."

Sally smiled at Mary. "His first name is Cheng. In China they give their last name first."

Cheng said, "Some young people use western tradition. My two aunts are here. They are very traditional. I better be correct, or they scold me."

The women asked questions and Cheng translated. "Where do you live?"

When Sally said they lived close to the Atlantic Ocean, the interpreter asked questions about fish. She described small fish and big boats for fishing. Then, whales, seals, purple clam shells for jewelry, and Canada geese. She mimed with her fingers how fast the small piping plover birds could run.

A warm feeling spread through Sally. She was standing with a group of locals and had been accepted. In Yangzhou, she had made friends with the people she worked with, and she had Han close by for support. Here she had done it on her own.

Mary pointed at her watch. It was time for their *hutong* tour.

"I need to go now," Sally told Cheng.

"You come again?" he asked. "They want more time with you."

Sally answered, "I hope so."

She looked at the women and waved goodbye. "Xiè xie."

MARY MET A COUPLE AT THE HOSTEL WHO HAD HIRED A private guide for a *hutong* tour. Roger and Cathleen Brown were from Hong Kong, and invited Mary and Sally to join them. The foursome took a taxi to the Drum and Bell Tower, the arranged meeting place that overlooked many of the old Beijing alleyways.

Yow Ming introduced herself and led them down a *hutong* alley. She told them she had been on the 2008 Olympics welcoming force. "I live in *hutong* neighborhood. City life rushed, always moving. In *hutong* I live in apartment on the street. More quiet and slow. I know my neighbors."

Ming continued to talk while they strolled along narrow roads. "Some Beijing *hutongs* date back to 13th century. Everything needed for everyday life can be found in alleyways and courtyards. Men ride three-wheel bikes with large boxes on back. Pick up trash, paper, metal, for recycle centers. Each have own bell signal to say what he picks up. They bring vegetables, eggs, chickens. People buy paper, needles and thread, a sack of coal."

She moved around bicycles, guiding them down an alley. "Everyone know everyone here. They practice Tai Chi in courtyards, in morning. Some still in pajamas! Night visits are outside, they play mahjong. There is butcher, barber and many cafés."

Two small children appeared in a doorway. Ming bent down to speak to them.

Later, she pointed to small boxes attached to the front walls of the buildings. "Can you guess what those are for?"

Mary said mail, Sally said newspapers, Roger and Cathleen shrugged their shoulders.

Ming shook her head and said "no". "It for milk delivery. No refrigerators here. Glass milk bottles have 8 or 16 ounces, left daily."

They passed a man washing clothes in a sink under a water pump. "Outdoor water sinks still used in *hutongs*. Community kitchens shared too." She opened a door to show a room with shelves and large woks over fire pits."

The end of the alley was ahead. Ming smiled and pointed to a stone building. "You must come see toilet."

They followed her into the long outhouse. On each side of the center aisle, a foot-wide trench ran down the length of the building. There was a continuous flow of water to flush. Men used the right side, women the left.

Sally stopped for a moment, transfixed. A woman was reading a book while squatting over the trench. There didn't seem to be the need for privacy Americans were so used to. "Are all the *hutongs* like this?" she asked the guide.

"I have western style toilet, water, and hot plate for cooking in apartment." Ming said.

Sally had seen other *hutong* neighborhoods during her travels. She was surprised to learn that many people like Ming lived in them with modern conveniences.

She popped a throat lozenge in her mouth and looked around for a café where they could stop. A cup of the drug store tea would be good. The streets were deserted. People worked during the day.

Mary remarked, "It's so clean! No trash in the street, no graffiti. It's obvious people are proud of their neighborhood."

Ming answered, "It is sad *hutongs* disappear. You are right, people have happy life here. Families here for generations. Builders tear down. Build tall residential and business complexes."

"Stalagmites," Sally added. "I see them everywhere. Tall apartments with no personality. Han said people from rural mountain towns are flooding the cities for work. Some work in the factories. And many work in construction to build more stalagmites.

"I read many *hutongs* were destroyed for the Olympics," Mary added.

"No one knows how many," Ming replied. "Estimate over 3,000 *hutong* neighborhoods destroyed and millions moved. Neighbors moved to different areas, lose security they had all their lives. Many relocated outside Beijing, transportation to jobs difficult or impossible. I take you for a visit with a woman in her *hutong* home."

They walked through a gate into a walled dirt courtyard with a tree, a hanging flower pot, a metal chair and a small round table. A smiling women met them at the door.

Inside the small room was a sofa, two chairs, and a TV on a table that did double duty as an eating area and desk. A double bed sat alone behind the sofa. A kitchen sink, a hot plate and a western toilet were in the same room and visible. A loft with boxes was overhead.

"Mrs. Chen live here since she marry. Her daughter want her to move in new condo. She won't go. Her friends here, she feels safe. She 84," Ming told the group.

Mrs. Chen served the group tea in paper cups. Sally was happy to drink the tea and relax while she listened to the guide translate Mrs. Chen's history on how she raised her family in one room.

The parents had slept on the bed in the back. Their three children slept in the narrow loft between the bed and the ceiling. A ladder sat in a corner. The oldest boy had married first. He and his wife slept on the double bed until they got their own home. The parents moved to the loft with the rest of the family. Then it was the next son's turn to marry and eventually leave. Mom and Dad were able to return to their downstairs bed. The daughter moved in with her husband's family.

Sally remembered thinking Frederick and Aimee's condo was small! There was much less space in this *hutong*. Yet, it somehow appealed to her. There was an intimacy with the bed in the main room. A vision of Han in the bed flashed through her mind. She liked it. Then she looked at the toilet. She didn't like that.

Mary asked, "What are you grinning about?"

"I was thinking about how ridiculous it would be to use the toilet in front of other people," Sally answered with a smirk.

"You look pale. Do you feel okay?" Mary asked. We should go back to the hostel."

"No, let's stay, we aren't far from the Olympic Village, and it's part of the tour." Sally stifled a cough.

A CITY BUS RIDE TOOK THE GROUP TO THE OLYMPIC Village. The Birds Nest and Water Cube were open for tours. The plaza where millions of tourists had walked was almost deserted. Sally thought the architectural wonders of the famous venues were awesome. But wondered about the cost. Twenty days of international good will had been exchanged for uprooting millions of residents. The *hutongs* had been home for generations.

Ming stopped to talk with a group of foreign visitors.

Sally's head throbbed. "I remember watching the opening ceremony on television in 2008. The sheer number of people made it seem magical. There were 2,008 Tai Chi masters, 2,008 drummers played bronze Fou drums, and 2,008 girls danced with parasols. The show lasted four hours."

Mary was standing in the Birds Nest stadium looking at the empty space in front of her. "They're going to do it again. In 2022, the Winter Olympics is scheduled for Beijing. I hope they don't destroy more *hutongs*."

"The smog is doing a number on me today," Sally coughed. "I'm having a hard time breathing. I need to go back to the hostel and rest."

"I told you before, we should go back. That bus ride wasn't good for you. In a crowded bus surrounded by exhaust fumes." Mary scolded.

They said good-bye to Roger and Cathleen, and "thank you" to Ming.

BACK AT THE HOSTEL, SALLY MADE A CUP OF HER prescription tea and went to her room. After she was comfortably ensconced on her bed she called Han to relate her day's adventure. "There was so much to learn about *hutong* life. My brain has information overload."

He asked, "Information overload? How that?"

Han's difficulty with English reminded her how laborious it was for him to translate her words and understand her feelings. She trusted him. But, she wondered, how much? She hadn't told him she was sick. "There is always more history for me to learn. More places to visit. More people."

"I take you on river boat in Guilin. You will have time for not learning," he said in a husky voice.

"Sometimes I feel there isn't much value to life here. There are so many people. So what if a few disappear? Even if it's millions. The *hutongs* were destroyed for just a few days of glory. The *concubines* and *eunichs* in the Forbidden City didn't have a choice of how they could live their lives."

Han's voice was sharp with tension. "My country have long history. Some parts sad. My life have sad. Do you see happy time in China? I show you parks with flowers. I have beautiful country. You see big city only. There is more."

Sally heard the hurt in his voice. She had insulted his home. "I'm sorry. You're right I don't know your country. I can't learn in just a few weeks. But I'm trying." A catch in her throat reminded her she was sick. "Maybe we should say goodnight now. I'm really tired."

The phone was silent. Then, in a low voice, he said, "I say goodnight. Call tomorrow. You are important person for me."

When she said goodnight, he had already ended the call. "What now?" she said to an empty room.

IN THE MORNING SALLY TOLD MARY SHE WANTED TO practice Tai Chi. "The women have peaceful energy, it will be good for me." She reassured Mary she was okay. "This might be my last chance to practice with them. We're leaving early tomorrow for our Great Wall tour."

She didn't have a lot of energy and the Tai Chi women seemed to know. They ended the form faster than the day before. Gentle touches on her arms showed concern. Without a translator, Sally didn't understand their words, but she could see the concern in their eyes. Allowing a sudden impulse, Sally hugged the woman closest to her, and found herself in an embrace with three others. Tears welled in her eyes. Her face was gently patted.

She looked at her new friends and wondered if her tears were for them, or for a man she had hurt in Shanghai. Han hadn't called her yet. And she felt bad about last night's awkward conversation. She slowly pulled herself away. After giving them a thumbs up she waved goodbye.

ALEXANDRA MET MARY AND SALLY AT THE CHINESE Cultural Center. They were enrolled in a two-hour landscape painting class, a recommended expat favorite. The center was dedicated to teaching Chinese culture, and sponsored classes and trips for expats and foreign visitors.

The classroom had two long tables covered with felt. A vertical strip of rice paper, three brushes, three dishes with colored ink, and a bowl of water were set out for each artist.

The teacher stood in the front of the room with a blank paper and a finished painting on the wall. Light came from a side window. The teacher's gentle voice, soothing odors of herbs and ink mixed in the air. Sally relaxed. A picture of clouds and mountains began to appear as she swirled colored water on the rice paper with slow strokes. All she had to do was allow her brush to move with the rhythm of her surroundings.

The class had six people. Everyone worked quietly as they painted the same scene, each with their own interpretation. Sally looked at her finished picture. "This is beautiful. I want to take another class."

While their pictures dried, the students moved to another room where they drank white, green and oolong tea. An earthy black tea was served at the end. Sally added honey to her tea to soothe her throat. The quiet morning felt good. Maybe she was almost over the flu.

She returned to the hostel with Mary. Their paintings were rolled up in soft cloth for packing.

"I'm going to take a nap." Sally said. "Tomorrow we're going to the Great Wall. I think I'll rest up for that." A walk on the Great Wall of China was, definitely, on her to do list. She wished she could breathe Cape Cod air. She hurt and wished her phone would ring with bird songs.

Mary gave her a stern look. "The phone works in both directions. You can push the button and say, 'Hello Han.'"

"What should I say? Do I apologize for saying what I believe is right?"

Sally's upbringing had stressed respect.

Her parents had come from different backgrounds. They had put their past behind them and honored the present.

Han answered immediately. "I happy you call. I remember you all day. Want to say hello."

Her heart was racing. "Han, I don't want to hurt you. I saw beautiful places in China and met good people. I would like to see more." She took a deep breath and added, "America has a past of shedding blood and hurting innocent people, too. When I spoke to you before, I forgot my own country's history."

Han sighed, "I sleep good tonight. We will have time in Guilin for more conversation."

The next day, Mary looked at Sally. "Your eyes are red. Are you sure you want to walk on the wall today? I don't like the way you look."

"I want to go," Sally answered. "The Great Wall of China was the one thing I wanted to see while here. The smog is awful here and it's hard to breathe. The air will be much better on top of the mountain." She popped a cough drop in her mouth, "These work."

Their plan was to be in a taxi to and from Mutianyu, a wall destination outside Beijing. Alexandra had told them the taxi driver was a great guide and would take them to a lesser known entrance. They could have lunch in a village café that served a popular steamed fish.

Sally was determined. "I'll only walk a little way on top of the wall. Don't worry about me. I'll have plenty of time later to rest. Come on, let's get something to eat before the guide gets here. He said he'd be here at 6:30."

THE CHEERFUL GUIDE INTRODUCED HIMSELF. "*NI HĂO*, I AM Tom, I bring you to wall. Very beautiful." He steered the cab around mopeds, buses and trucks. "We come to wall at place with less people, early morning. You see wall on top of mountains far away."

They traveled on a busy road for an hour, and passed roadside stands selling small replica portions of the wall.

The parking lot was almost empty when they arrived. They left Tom and started up a path. Souvenir stalls were opening to sell tee shirts with dragons and lettering; "*I Walked On The Great Wall Of China.*" Sally walked slowly. Her chest hurt. The dirt path moved uphill to a break in the wall.

Sally stood enthralled at the perfect view of the wall as it climbed up and down green mountain ridges. It looked like a path had been cut across steep forbidding terrain. She could see for miles and miles. From where she stood, civilization didn't exist.

A strong wind whistled across the stones making eerie sounds, she heard voices in the wind. Soldiers from the past. Except for four or five Chinese men and women, they were alone. She became part of her surroundings and drifted back into history to a time when men stood on this wall to protect their homeland from invaders.

There had been a great human toll in building the wall. Workers did not live long. They didn't volunteer. Many were forced into labor. The wall had been built with blood and tears. Families had mutilated their sons to make them unable to work. To keep them alive.

Suddenly Sally felt dizzy. Her head felt heavy. The gray stones and green tree tops blurred. She took a step but her stomach felt queasy. She reached for the stone rampart edge. A crunch in her right ankle. "Mary!"

When Sally opened her eyes, Mary was looking down at her. "Don't move! You hit your head! Where's your phone?"

"Ouch! What happened? Phone's in my leg pocket. My head hurts." Sally moved her hand toward her leg. "There's blood on my hand!"

Mary had Sally's phone and pressed the white button. "I'm calling Han. I don't think anyone speaks English here."

Faces peered down at her with concerned eyes. They chatted in Chinese. Sally felt her stomach turn over. "I'm going to throw up!" She tried to turn to her side and felt hands help her move.

"Han, it's Mary. Sally's hurt. We're on the Great Wall. She passed out and fell. She's really white. She's been sick." Mary listened, then said, "No one speaks English here."

Sally reached for the phone.

"She wants to talk to you." Mary held it for her.

"I'm scared Han." Sally's voice was plaintiff. "My ankle really hurts, and my head too. I cut it somewhere."

A man came up and pointed at the phone and then himself. Sally held the phone out to the stranger.

After a conversation with Han, the man handed the phone back to Mary. He sent a boy running down the path.

Mary nodded a thank you to the man and listened to Han. "Okay, I'll call you when we get to the doctor." She held the phone to Sally again. "Open your eyes. You hit your head. You might have a concussion. Here, Han wants to talk to you."

Han's voice was a comfort. "They go for chair to carry you. They bring you to doctor. Man knows good doctor in Mutianyu. Do not worry. Stop phone now so battery will keep."

Two men came jogging across the wall. They held a traditional *sedan* chair between them. Tom followed behind with an elderly, overweight woman. She carried a cloth bag. When they got to Sally, the woman immediately barked orders to everyone.

Bending over Sally, she stuck out her tongue. Sally understood and stuck out her tongue. This was something she had done at home in the acupuncturist's office. The woman wrapped a cloth around Sally's head and instructed the chair carriers to lift Sally.

"I can stand." Sally began to sit up.

"I think she knows what she's doing. Let her direct traffic," Mary said and moved to stand next to the chair. "Han told me to get you to a doctor."

Tom said, "We go to village doctor. I bring help."

"This is so embarrassing." Sally sat in the chair. "This is the kind of seat they carried the emperor on."

Mary laughed.

The village hospital had one room. Men in white jackets moved about the room, carefully inserting needles in the feet, arms, and legs of patients lying on tables in cubicles separated with cloth curtains. It was quiet, and it looked like some people were asleep.

After another tongue exam, one of the men checked Sally's pulse. He stuck needles in her feet and arms. A cloth bandage was wrapped around her ankle. Blood was cleaned from her head and a cold cloth laid over her cut. An herbal tea was brought for Sally to drink.

Mary used Sally's phone to call Han again and handed it to the doctor.

Sally was feeling drowsy when the doctor gave her the phone.

Han's strained voice sounded far away. "The acupuncturist place needles to keep energy flow after head injury. He say you will be well, foot not broke. You have sick chest. He give you medicine for chest. You need rest." He searched for words. "I feel pain for you."

"Han, I feel better. I guess I should have told you I was sick earlier. I didn't want to worry you. I miss you."

"You go to hospital in Beijing. Eastern doctor make sure. I talk to you more in hostel. I talk to Mary now." Han's voice cracked.

Mary took the phone. She nodded, smiled and said "*yes*" several times before she hung up. "Come on, don't fall asleep, the tea is supposed to relax you and help you breathe, not put you to sleep! Tom is ready to bring us back to Beijing.

SALLY HOBBLED INTO THE HOSTEL ON CRUTCHES. AFTER AN x-ray, the doctor at the Beijing clinic said the ankle was only sprained. He had seen patients use the herbal tea for congestion and told Sally he believed it worked. If not, she was to come back for an antibiotic. She didn't need an appointment, he explained. When people got sick, they simply went to the doctor and were seen in the order they arrived.

In their hostel room, Sally looked at her friend. "Guess I screwed up our visit to the wall. I'm sorry."

"I should have remembered you don't handle sick well." Mary shook her head. "You scared me. And Han. I had a difficult time understanding him, he was rambling in English and Chinese."

Sally looked apologetic. "I feel better after the acupuncture treatment and I'm hungry. We missed lunch."

"They have soup on the hostel menu," Mary said. "No beer for you while you're drinking your tea concoction." She shrugged and looked into Sally's eyes. "Who cares about the Great Wall? There's lots of stone walls in New England I can visit."

Sally spent the afternoon reading in the hostel lobby. She had her foot propped up on a stool. After a dinner of rice and chicken soup, she sighed and said, "Let's go for a walk. I've been sitting forever."

Mary looked at her watch. "Let's let dinner settle first."

"What are you talking about? Let dinner settle? I'm not talking about going swimming." Sally laughed at the ridiculous statement. Mary was acting strange. She kept looking at the door. Well, she didn't need Mary to go for a walk and began to stand.

Mary pointed to the door, so Sally turned to look.

Han walked in and said, "Bullet train from Shanghai fast."

Mary ran to him and gave him a hug. "I'm really happy you're here." She looked at Sally. "She won't admit it, but she's scared. And a difficult patient."

"I don't like being sick." Sally struggled to get up. The wrap on her leg made standing awkward.

Han reached her with several fast steps. He leaned over to give her a gentle hug. "I need to see you okay. I stay tonight. Go back to school tomorrow. I want to take you to doctor first. Must get you well." His clothes were rumpled, and his hands shook. "Visitors get sick in Beijing. Bad air." He paused to examine her head and wrapped ankle. "I must be here with you."

"I'll leave you two alone," Mary said. "I want to explore the neighborhood. Han, you're in charge now."

Sally looked at Han. A five hour train ride was an investment and said so much more than any words he might speak. "I guess I overdid it, traveling around so much. I didn't want to be sick, so I didn't say anything." She stopped to look at him, "You're here!"

They sat down. He put his arm around her and pulled her close to his chest. "I worry my past make you sick."

Her head on his shoulder, she looked down at their clasped hands. In a shaky voice she asked, "Can we still go on the boat ride in Guilin? I made myself sick. I didn't rest enough."

"Yes, we go. Air is good there. Boat on River Li gentle. I come back to Beijing and go there on plane with you."

She snuggled close. "I feel much better now."

Later, in their room, Sally asked Mary, "Did you know he was coming?"

Mary nodded and smiled, "Yes, he told me over the phone when we were at the clinic. He made the arrangements right after you talked to him from the wall. He asked me not to tell you." Mary paused to study Sally. "He's special, you know. He had to make arrangements for his class, get reservations on the train and for an overnight here. He didn't even go home to pack. He left right from school."

"He knows about Michael. I told him." Sally looked at Mary, "It bothers him that I'm married. But he came anyway. I'm so confused! I have feelings for this man, *and* I'm still committed to Michael. I always will be."

Mary sat on the bed next to Sally and gave her a hug. "Stop worrying. It won't help. Relax and get better. The trip to Guilin sounds great. You will have plenty of time to think about everything when you get home."

In the morning, Han brought Sally to an acupuncturist. Then to a Hilton hotel near her hostel. "This good place for you to rest. Have clean air-conditioned lounge. I must take train back to Shanghai. I will call you." He kissed her forehead, and then with a sad face he turned and left.

SALLY SPENT THE NEXT TWO DAYS DRINKING TEA AND GOING for more acupuncture treatments. One morning she and Mary went to another painting class and an afternoon massage. Her strength returned, and she began to walk without crutches.

Bird calls signaled Han's daily phone calls. She listened to his deep voice, that become alluring to her ears. When she looked at his face on the phone she saw desire in his eyes. Each day brought her closer to their trip to Guilin. She wondered if he could see and feel her anticipation over the phone.

ON THE NIGHT OF THE EMBASSY DINNER, SALLY PUT ON her red dress.

"You look stunning in that dress," Mary said.

"Thanks! I wore this dress on a special dinner date with Han in Yangzhou. I wish he were here."

"You're going to be with him in two days. Right? I think you should go to Yangzhou for a year. You raved about the children. And you already made friends there. Han told me he could live there. He wants to be with you," Mary grinned.

Sally frowned, "I don't know. I miss home. But something about China and Han tugs at me." She turned to Mary and smiled. "I'll have time to think when I'm home. Let's have fun tonight. We should go to the lobby to wait for the taxi."

AT THE GATE TO THE BRITISH EMBASSY THEY WERE welcomed by guards in elaborate uniforms. Their taxi door was opened with a slight bow. Flower beds were arranged on the grounds to look like palace gardens. The air smelled fresh. There seemed to be less smog on the tree-lined avenue where many embassies stood. There was less traffic.

Alexandra met them with hugs. She introduced her handsome husband, William. He was exactly what Sally expected. Tall with a dashing mustache, and firm handshake. He winked at Sally and said, "I heard about you."

She laughed. Her foot was still tender, but her chest felt much better. Her cough was almost gone.

The four-course dinner was served on royal china. Baked potatoes, roast beef, and roasted vegetables were cooked in an oven, all tasted delicious. Sally was again reminded of the difference between cultures. Savoring the familiar taste of a roast, Sally wondered if she could live for a year without an oven to roast or bake her meals.

After dessert, Alexandra pulled Mary and Sally into a side room for girl talk. "Sally are you going to come back to China?" Alexandra asked. "I hope you do. I'll visit Yangzhou and we can go on trips together through the Cultural Center."

Mary added, "And I can come again. I would have someone to visit in Beijing and in Yangzhou."

"I don't know." Sally shook her head. "Getting sick scared me. I was lucky to have Han to help me after I fell." She looked at her friends. "I need to go home. Leaving Han is going to be hard. I like him . . . a lot. And, I really enjoyed teaching the children. But we have our differences. I hurt him when I talked about China's violent past. I didn't mean to, but I did. I can't shake off the differences in our lives."

Alexandra said, "I have found Chinese men are sincere and honorable. Han was there for you when you needed him. You won't regret spending time with him." She pointed to Sally's outfit. "And you wear a Chinese dress with such ease. The dress and your blond curls are perfect together. If you decide to live here, you'll be more comfortable once you understand Mandarin."

A taxi was waiting at the embassy gate. Sally gave Alexandra a hug and said, "Thank you. You're right, we will have fun together if I do come back. But I probably won't see you again before I go home. I'll email."

MARY LEFT FOR CAPE COD WITH A SUITCASE FULL OF GIFTS. Sally's purple backpack was ready. She planned to meet Han at the airport. The brochures of Guilin advertised the city as "Romantic." Her heart raced as she headed for the airport.

9

BEIJING

HAN

Han sat back in his seat. Five hours on the bullet train and he would be in Beijing. Then a plane, with Sally, to Guilin. He had a week to convince her to come back to him. Students and teachers in Yangzhou wanted her to return. Nobody wanted her to return more than he did.

Students in Shanghai said, "You are different, tell funny stories." A teacher had added, "You wear new clothes. You look hot!" He walked with a bounce.

He wanted to put his arms around her again. Her yellow hair curled around his fingers when he held her head and kissed her. She looked at him with round brown eyes that were sometimes golden. Her smooth arms moved with slow determination when they practiced Tai Chi. Her hands were soft, like silk, when his fingers reached for hers. He wanted more time. He felt young again.

Frederick said, "Bring her back here. The children ask for her.

She talked to them about her life in America. They told her about their home. In one week they formed a bond."

Han had a contract from the school to teach English and give history lectures. He would live in Yangzhou and bring her to a park every day to see the flowers. He remembered her arms around him on the moped. Her hands on his chest.

Aimee's advice, "Hold her. Be romantic. Show her you care." He smiled when he remembered how Aimee had showed him how to hold Sally.

Mary told him, "She likes it here, but she's afraid. Let her know she won't be alone. It's okay to take care of her. She wanted you when she fell. I'll talk to her, I'll help."

He wanted to cook for her and watch her eat. Sometimes she hid bones in a napkin. She didn't think he knew this. It was hard for him not to laugh, she was so damn cute.

The first time he saw her, she had walked into his life with American confidence and quickly became a necessary addition. He smiled with the memory and looked down at his hands. He wanted to hold her then.

GUILIN IS A BEAUTIFUL CITY ON THE LI RIVER IN southern China. Its warm weather nourishes flowers and trees, where birds live and sing. The river current moves slowly. Sometimes it gurgles over rock shelves built by local fishermen. Boatmen use long-handled poles to pull their bamboo rafts up river. They sing as they paddle. He would sing to her, too.

He remembered the last time he had been to Guilin. He had brought his wife to rest. She was so fragile and brave. There wasn't much time left. He had held her close to him in bed, thinking maybe he could keep her forever, if he didn't let go. It was three years ago. He was ready for a new future.

He made reservations at a secluded hotel that overlooked the Li River. Not a hostel, a nice hotel. They would enjoy days and nights of clean air, good food. There would be time to talk. He had a plan.

Han sent a text to Frederick. "Mr. Romantic has arrived at the airport. Sally is waving."

10

GUILIN

SALLY

A taxi from the Guilin airport brought Sally and Han to a hotel overlooking the Li River. Flowers surrounded the buildings. Stone pathways led to secluded benches. Warm fragrant air and quiet solitude welcomed Sally.

Her room had a double bed with a soft mattress and embroidered bedspread. It was so much better than a pad in hostels. There were yellow decorative pillows, a straw mat on the floor, and landscape paintings of the River Li hung on the walls. An electric kettle to boil and sterilize drinking water sat on a bureau across from the bed. A round table and two chairs were outside her door.

A young girl showed her the room with a smile, "Good room. Wedding here two days. You will see." Sally remembered going to weddings of friends and work colleagues. Wedding styles had changed over the years.

Hans' room was next door. If the wedding took place outside

their rooms, could they participate? It would feel strange to share such an intimate time with strangers. But the idea was also exciting. She wondered what a Chinese wedding would look like.

After she unpacked, Sally went outside to find Han. He was talking to a young man and waved for her to join them. She told him, "My room is beautiful! This place is amazing. I hope we can explore a little."

Han smiled. "Here is Chang. He works for hotel. There is wedding here. You want to see wedding? Very happy time."

"Yes! I want to see." She looked at Chang and said *ni hāo,* "You have a beautiful hotel."

"He speak little English." Han's eyes twinkled. "He bring us to bench to see river. Not far for walking. Is foot good for walking?"

Sally looked at the two men watching her with concerned eyes. "Yes, I can walk. I want to spend time outdoors," She assured them.

Chang led them to a bench overlooking the river. It was surrounded by bougainvillea and lush green plants. After he made sure they were both comfortably seated, Chang had a brief conversation with Han, nodded, and left.

Sally took several deep breaths of the perfumed air. "Do you have instructions from friends on how we should spend our time together? Mary, Juno, and Alexandra sent e-mails, and said I should let things happen."

"Be romantic!" Han laughed. "I hear that from Frederick, Aimee, and Mary." He put his arm around her. His hand held her shoulder. "How am I doing?"

Sally felt herself tremble at his touch. She was anxious because she didn't know what would happen. Or, more important, what she wanted to happen. A plane reservation for a flight from Shanghai to Boston was in her bag. She was leaving China in six days.

Romance was in the air. His hair was neatly cut and his eyes . . . dreamy. His cotton shirt was open at the neck and Sally could see a bit of his bare chest. There was something different about Han today. He stretched his legs out in front of him and crossed his feet. A relaxed, confident pose.

Sally answered his question. "Sure is a good start. This place is paradise."

They were alone. No horns blaring from the city streets. The path in front of them was clear. The air was clean. Chang brought cold beer and steamed dumplings and set them on a side table. Paradise!

In the river below, a man wearing a wide brimmed straw hat stood on a small bamboo raft. He seemed to be pounding the water with a paddle.

"What is he doing? He's beating the water." Sally asked.

"Fishing. Noise stun fish, they come up top. He scoop with net."

The man slammed and scooped at the river with a long pole and net. He was not wearing a life jacket. His long-sleeved shirt and loose pants moved around him with the gentle breeze.

Sally asked, "Why isn't he afraid of falling in the river?"

"His job. Every day fish, river his home. In America, how they fish?"

"In big boats on the ocean. Sometimes they go out on the boats for days. Commercial fishing requires licenses and there are rules about how many fish and sometimes how many weeks they can fish. They use nets that drag behind the boats to catch fish."

She paused. "They use smaller boats for sport or hobby. Sometimes they sit down while they fish and use fishing poles. They wear life jackets."

"We go river boat ride. You will see birds fish." Han smiled. Conversation was easy.

"Cormorants. I read about them. They catch fish but don't eat them." Sally remembered the birds from her pre-trip reading.

"They eat fish. Fisherman take good care of bird. You will see."

After a lazy afternoon enjoying the resort's serenity, they walked to the outdoor dining pavilion a limited menu featuring daily specials. They could take a van into town for dinner but decided to stay where they were. Why go where there were tons of people again? A savory dinner of white rice, chicken pieces with bones, and spicy bok choy became romantic as they were the only customers.

Sally watched as Han engaged the staff in conversations for local sightseeing ideas. Heads nodded. After several long monologues, Han turned to Sally. "We have plan for rice terrace visit. Go tomorrow. Is that good?"

"Yes. I think there is a picture in my room of the fields. It looks like colored ribbons."

"Plant rice fields for mountain shape. Have water irrigation. Each field belong to one family. We may see them work. Guide take us to Golden Buddha Peak to see Jinkeng-terraced fields. There is cable ride to top. Less walking." Han grinned as he described the rice fields.

After their meal had been cleared, a young waiter talked with Han. "He ask do you want practice night QiGong with staff?" Han said, "I tell him you have hurt foot. He say will be good."

As they watched the staff clear tables and chairs from the pavilion area for QiGong practice Sally looked at Han. She decided he was a friend magnet. Wherever they went, he easily made conversation.

Stars began to appear in the night sky. Sally looked at them wistfully. "It's been a while since I've seen stars." And then she looked at Han. "Yes, I want to practice. Will you help me?"

With lips slightly curved in a smile, transforming an otherwise serious face, he moved closer to her. "Yes, I take care of you."

Sally gave him a shove and they both laughed. She looked up at the twinkling stars again. Life was good.

The QiGong practice was led by Chang. They stood outside the pavilion and were joined by staff members. Sally saw the girl who had brought her to her room. Two older women joined the group. She stood next to Han and followed Chang's graceful moves.

The QiGong practice was slow. One of the members stopped after a few minutes and began to play a flute. Han kept his eyes on Sally. When she began to tire, he took her hand to bring her back to their rooms.

At the door to her room, he pulled her close and kissed her. His kiss was firm, his hands held her head and the back of her neck. She felt her body tremble. Yes! He was being romantic. "Good dreams!" he whispered in her ear.

Her legs were shaking, and not from a sore foot, she said good night. This was a new side of Han, and she wanted more of him.

She lay on her bed and wondered what Han was going to do next.

"*Have you forgotten me?*" Michael intruded into her thoughts.

She would be home soon. And she would go to the hospital to see Michael. Once again, tears filled her eyes when she thought about her husband. He had no life, only a hospital bed. His body had shrunk over the years. He didn't eat. Nourishment was delivered by a tube to his stomach. His eyes were closed, he didn't see the bare walls of his room. The doctors had told her he didn't have pain. She wondered if he felt her hand holding his.

Sally wiped at her tears with a fist. There would be time enough later for crying. She was here for only a few more days. Then she would leave China. And Han!

A breakfast of dumplings, watermelon triangles, and tea was served on the table outside their rooms.

"This is luxury." Sally looked at Han. "I watched the sunrise. It was lovely."

Han smiled. "We watch sunset over rice fields. Best time for photographs."

Chang brought the hotel van to a stop in front of the pavilion. He got out and introduced a second couple to Sally and Han. Melie and Lee Chan were on their honeymoon and lived in Beijing. They were sharing the Longsheig County excursion. It was a two and a half hour drive to the Huangluo village and terraced rice fields.

AFTER A STOP IN GUILIN TO BUY STRAW HATS FOR THEIR day in the sun, they returned to their seats in the van. Melie and Lee spoke little English, and Han took over the job as translator. Sally recognized an occasional Mandarin word. She knew *mēili* meant beautiful, *hǎo* was good, and *xiè xie* was thank you.

The van pulled up to a hotel beside a wide stream. A village built on stilts could be seen on the other side of the stream. A rugged mountain behind the village.

"Rice fields other side mountain. We have lunch, cross bridge for Huangluo Village." Han said as he pointed across the road at a rickety bridge.

Sally wondered if she wanted to cross over on the wood bridge. "We're going to walk on that? It looks scary."

"You want me carry you?" Han grinned and raised his eyebrows.

Sally laughed, "Thanks but I can walk. My foot feels much better."

Wood planks had been placed across ropes. The bridge swayed when they crossed. Fortunately, there was also a rope waist high to hold onto, but it was still scary, and she took baby steps on the planks. She gripped Han's arm.

"Must let blood come for arm," He teased, but stayed close to her.

A VILLAGE OF 80 HOMES BUILT ON STILTS SNUGGED UP TO the mountain. Each house was three stories. Chickens and donkeys were protected from rain and snow with the floor of the second story where food and provisions were kept safe from unwanted scavengers. Families lived on the third floor, above the dust and odors. The main street of the village had tables with vendors selling embroidered cloth for pillows and tablecloths. Intricate designs of birds, flowers and dragons had been sewn with silk thread. Sally found a square with a dragon she would have made into a pillow when she got home.

Sally and Han visited a show translated into English that explained the long hair tradition of the Red Yao women. They grew their silky black hair to lengths of 1.7 meters, close to 6 feet. Single girls covered their hair with a blue scarf, saving the beautiful hair for their husbands to see first on their wedding day. Married women wore their hair twisted in a rope and coiled on top of their head in a tray style. If there was a small bun at the front, she was a mother. No bun, she was married but didn't have children. Because they were a minority culture, they could have more than one child. The Red Yao women claimed their beautiful silky hair was due to rice water. The water they used to rinse rice was also used to bathe their hair.

The van took them to the back of the mountain, and the Jinkeng Terraces. Sally pressed her nose to the window glass as the van passed the rice fields. She could see why the rice terraces were considered among the most fantastic scenery in all of China. There were 25 square miles of terraced fields that wound up the mountain in tiered bands, an ingenious irrigation system for the scarce land and water.

"They farm since Yuan Dynasty. Families grow rice for generations." Han held her hand as they looked up the mountain steps.

Sally was entranced. "The colors of the earth and fields blend and then separate with each terrace set higher. It's a beautiful nature painting."

"We go to top on cable car. Small walk. You see sun move down mountain. Each terrace shine. Very beautiful."

Sally forgot to take pictures. Each moment on the mountain was too precious to get distracted fidgeting with a camera.

HAN JUMPED UP FROM THEIR BREAKFAST TABLE. HIS EYES were on something behind Sally. She turned to see a young man walking toward them with a determined stride. He held a red envelope and, when he reached Han, he used both hands to extend the envelope with a bow. Han accepted it with both hands and a return bow.

"He invite us for wedding banquet today. Do you want to go?" Han asked.

"Yes! I want to go. What an honor."

She turned to the smiling youth and said, "*Xiè xie*, I am honored to come to your wedding." Then a look at Han, "What time?"

The man looked embarrassed. In English he said, "We have banquet here." Then he added something in Chinese.

Han continued the conversation with head nods and smiles. He told Sally, "We not go to marriage. They have traditional ceremony, go to registry office for paper. We go to party for family and friends. Tonight. Many people."

Sally's eyes opened wide. This was a surprise. What would she wear?

"We go shop for red envelope wedding gift. I get moped." Han looked happy, his face glowed.

"I sent my red dress home with Mary. I don't have anything

to wear." Sally was talking too fast. Her breakfast food was forgotten. She was going to a wedding, she had to get ready and she had nothing dressy to wear.

"Bride wear red dress," Han answered with a grin. "You are beautiful. Have blond curls."

"Thank you. But I better wear more than blond curls," she gave Han a shy smile.

Morning Tai Chi practice on the path near their favorite bench helped mellow Sally's mounting anxiety. She thought about being a guest at a Chinese wedding. There were so many customs in this country she knew nothing about. What was the meaning of the red envelope, and what if she made some kind of cultural blunder? One good thing, she didn't need to worry about saying something wrong. Except, just because she didn't understand Mandarin didn't mean they didn't understand English. More to worry about. She focused on her Tai Chi practice. Soon she would put her arms around Han on a moped and "let things happen."

A consultation with hotel staff resulted in a borrowed moped and directions to a wedding supply shop.

"We get red envelope for marriage gift. Woman will borrow you dress. She will fix hair and makeup. Do you want?" Han came close to touch her hair. "Man say bride ask for pictures with yellow hair. I borrow clothes too."

Sally felt a sudden weakness in her knees and took a step back to maintain her balance. The man next to her, inside her personal space, was emitting romantic vibes. She began to tremble. A thought raced through her mind. Michael, help me! What if it happens again? Another accident?

"He is not me. Trust him. It's time."

THEY RODE PAST SHOPS TO A STREET OF OLD STONE BLOCK buildings. Han found a parking spot in front of a small shop. Red lanterns hung from the ceiling, yellow banners splashed across the walls. Cut out dragon decorations and souvenir post-cards were piled on tables. A Siamese cat stood in the back of the room.

The shop proprietor met them at the door. She wore a blue flowered dress and introduced herself. "Hello, I am Lee. Do you come for wedding clothes? Chang call me."

Han replied, "Yes, I need shirt and pants and Sally needs dress.

"I go find clothes," Lee replied with a frown. "You are very tall, maybe not have good dress for you." She shook her head and disappeared behind a curtain in the back of the store.

Sally walked over to the cat and bent down. "Hello. What is your name?" The cat came and rubbed against her. "I'll call you Sasha. Is that okay?"

"*Meow.*" Sasha turned to go behind a dresser.

Sally followed. A basket on the floor held two kittens.

"Sasha, you're a mama! What adorable babies."

One of the kittens crawled out of the basket and nestled in Sally's hand. She held the kitten next to her chest and felt him purr. "Han! Look at this adorable kitten. My cat at home, Sasha, looked just like this, when she was a baby."

Lee, who barely reached Han's shoulder, peered at Sally over gold-rimmed glasses. "He like you. You hold him." She grinned at Han and nodded her head.

Sally didn't fit into the "borrow clothes." It was decided a blouse and skirt from her school clothes collection, with a yellow silk sash for her waist would look good. She held the kitten on her lap while her hair was piled on her head with a shell comb. Dark eye makeup made her round eyes look larger. Sasha sat next to Sally's chair while they drank tea and Han modeled a yellow brocade jacket. The kitten purred. Sasha looked up at Sally, then she turned and returned to her baby behind the bureau.

Han looked at Sally with a twinkle in his eyes, a slight smile.

After Sally purchased several red paper lanterns that came folded in envelopes to bring home, they got ready to leave the shop. Han's jacket, and her yellow sash were carefully folded and placed in plastic protective bags for the trip back to the hotel. She returned the kitten to the basket. He tried to stay in her hand, and she found herself not wanting to let him go. Sasha said, "*Meow*."

Sally smiled at the cats and said, "Good-bye Sasha."

Han piled their purchases into the mopeds' side storage containers for the return trip to the hotel. He was slow in arranging the bags and boxes.

"Wait!" Lee came running with a bamboo box for Sally. "From Sasha," she said. A baby "*meow*" came from inside the box. Tiny blue eyes peered up at her from a small window. Before she knew what was happening the box was secured to the back of the moped and Han was speeding them back to the hotel.

"He's the cutest thing I ever saw." Sally watched the kitten explore her room. "Is it okay to have him here? I wish I could bring him home with me. But that's impossible."

The girl who had been caring for her room brought a small

box of sand. She left and returned with bowls of water and food for the kitten.

Han watched the kitten. He looked at Sally and said, "He stay Shanghai with me. You come back to us."

She was leaving so much behind, butterflies sprang into action in her stomach. "Don't make me cry, it will ruin my makeup. What happens now?"

"We go marriage banquet."

The newlyweds posed for photos in front of Sally and Han's special garden bench. The couple radiated love in the romantic ambiance. Sally looked into Han's eyes, and thought, "He feels it too."

The bride wore a red satin dress with gold embroidery. Gold beads sparkled in her hair and she carried a bouquet of red and white flowers. The groom wore a red silk jacket with gold embroidered trim over a white shirt and white pants.

"She looks like a porcelain doll," Sally whispered to Han. His arm was around her waist. "I guess we missed the wedding."

"They pose for photos before marry. Have tea ceremony with parents. Marry official in registry office, then have banquet. Family and friends wait for after. She wear more dresses. Some modern women wear white dress for banquet."

"Why do they change?"

"Red traditional for marriage. Means love, luck, and happiness. White is mourning color. Western culture introduce white marriage dress to young people. They use old and new ideas."

"I wore a red dress for our dinner in Yangzhou and I was happy." She blushed with the memory of his arms around her and the goodnight kiss.

"I always happy when we together," Han answered.

Sally looked down at the river. No-one was fishing, the water tumbled across rocks and continued its journey downstream. She had a Chinese wedding dress in America and a new kitten in China. In between was a man. Han had made a difference in her life and now she had one foot in America and the other here. How did this happen?

She had come to China for one week with Mary. It had been easy for her to fall in love with vacation destinations in the past, but home had always beckoned. The salt water on her feet washed away any leftover travel bugs. Her purple backpack would go back in her bedroom closet. She felt tears well up. She hated "Goodbyes."

The photographer asked Sally to pose for pictures with the bride and groom. A blond curl moment. She would forever be in a stranger's wedding album.

THEY STOOD AT THE GIFT TABLE IN FRONT OF THE BANQUET. Han presented their red envelope with both hands in a formal gesture. The envelope collector recorded something on a sheet in front of her. He took her hand to enter the banquet.

They sat at a table near their hotel rooms and watched the married couple visit each table and drink with their guests. The bride now wore a white silk dress with pink flowers. The groom had on a white suit. Sally noticed the bride was taking only tiny sips of wine as she greeted guests. There were many tables of guests for them to visit.

Children darted among the guests. A wedding was an occasion enjoyed by family members of all ages. Grandmothers wore traditional dress and teenage girls had on mini-skirts.

Food was plentiful. There were buffet tables with continuous additions of more dishes. Sally kept a napkin handy to hide the bones. Her wine glass never seemed to be empty. She listened to nearby conversations but understood little. Fortunately, Han made it easy for her. He translated, he held her hand and poured more wine.

After dark, fireworks lit up the sky. The loud bang of fire-crackers made Sally worry about the kitten alone in her room.

"Han, I want us to go to my room. We need to be with the kitten."

"I take off my borrow jacket and come. Good idea."

When Sally opened the door to her room the kitten ran to greet her. She took off her party clothes and put on a tee shirt and pants. Then sat on her bed. The kitten jumped and rolled with a scarf she waved around him.

Han knocked and came in carrying a bottle of wine, two glasses, and a red ball for the baby. He had also changed into casual pants and a tee shirt.

A ball game on the floor entertained the adults and tired the kitten. He soon curled up on the floor and fell asleep. Han poured wine and they sat up on the bed together. Sally caught the subtle scent of lavender. The air in the room seemed to glow with a mellow seduction.

"Our kitten needs a name. You name him, Han." She paused, then added, "And I think you should stay here tonight to keep us company."

"Li good name for him, mean strong like river. I stay."

He put their wine glasses on a side table and turned out the light. Moonlight spilled into the room from a side window. Han pulled her close.

Except for his breath, the room was quiet.

"A patter of rain, fluttering wings, musk. Colors floating on a pool, silent springs rising to arcs, then rainbows. A bubble of gold grew to crimson. Wait for it . . .wait for it. . . a burst of energy. Chinese fireworks.

A whispered voice. "Wait, American girl."

"More," she said.

His lips on her eyelids, his heat now gentle, butterfly wings. Her hands trembling with chi energy. Firm on his chest. His muscles moving with a life of their own, knowing her strength.

Holding him tight she moved one hand lower, waited. His breath allowed for more, she moved still lower. He surged to meet her, grasping her hand to lay it on journey's end.

More. She knew him now, her kisses followed the trail she had made on his chest, stomach, along his hips. He smelled of a day's sweat. The tip of her tongue reached his salty flesh. The rhythm of his heart pulsated her blood. He was hers.

A pearl grew; protected and cherished, it gleamed with a healthy glow. His eyes were steady, holding hers. "Now!" he said.

His hands circled her, and with an athlete's grace he moved and she was under him. One hand found her breast. "You are mine!" he said and claimed his prize. When her hand reached for his face, he grasped her palm and, one at a time, tasted her fingers. Her back arched, muscles responding to his commands.

She called out, heard her own voice, an echo. Another sound: a murmur, not words, the language a body knows, feels, remembers.

Sally felt their heat still on the sheets. His scent, slick, wet, a crumpled white pile, no longer innocent. She brought it to her face and remembered. The blanket on the floor seemed forgotten, alone. A pillow across the room, part of a long-ago game".

A morning sun seeped in around the window curtain.

"Han?"

He lay next to her in the bed. Had it all been a dream?

He pulled her into his arms. She wasn't dreaming now.

Breakfast at their outdoor table in rumpled clothes brought satisfied grins from staff. Sally was happy and smiled at the girl who brought their food.

"You need to fess up about Li. You knew there were Siamese kittens at that store yesterday, didn't you?" Sally teased.

"Fess up?" Han raised his eyebrows. His eyes a mirthful twinkle.

"Tell the truth."

"American slang interesting. I always tell you truth. Mei found kittens on computer. She say Sasha kitten, teach children, and maybe Han bring you back China. Does that work for you?" He raised an eyebrow and studied her eyes.

"She may be right. But did you also plan on us attending a wedding?"

"I plan bring you store for shopping. Wedding surprise gift for me. Hotel have many wedding banquets. Waiter suggest groom invite romantic people."

An awkward silence followed as Sally remembered their night together . . .

AFTER MICHAEL'S ACCIDENT THERE HAD BEEN OTHER MEN. She wasn't good at relationships, something always happened to end them. Michael had been her soul mate and that hideous car crash had taken him from her, in an instant. At first, she had hated living alone, but eventually she accepted it. Later, she decided it was safer than taking a chance on experiencing the pain of another loss.

She looked at Han and in a shy voice said, "I'm scared. Last night felt so right. I've been living like a widow for five years. I feel loved again with you. Everything is different here, I don't know the relationship rules. What happens next? I'm going home in three days."

Han reached for her hand. "I have no woman for three years. When I saw you with Tai Chi in Shanghai, I knew. It was my birthday, you were gift. I have surprise when I see you have blond curls. I decide to keep you. Your smile and eyes make me happy. My wife would have liked you, she approve."

She felt tears rising. "Can you come to America to visit? So we can spend more time together?"

"Visa for me difficult. China my home," his eyes were downcast.

"I know. I asked in Beijing. I can travel back and forth easily, but you can't."

She began folding a napkin into squares, food still on her plate. Her breath came fast, her heart raced, a sudden chill making her body shake.

Han saw her stress, he wanted to help her, "Important we practice Tai Chi now." He put his tea cup down, pushed his chair back, and stood. He held out his hand.

"The food, our clothes?" Sally asked.

"Staff knows, Li knows, we come back." Han answered with reassuring confidence.

At their Tai Chi practice area Sally followed his forms. The morning exercise allowed her mind to relax and empty of all thought. The simple moves were muscle memory, one moment at a time. At first she was stiff without balance, her mind and body disconnected. But she stayed with Han, trusting him to help her heal. Gradually her shoulders relaxed, her neck turned, her legs obeyed, and time disappeared. They were silently joined by two waiters from last night's banquet. Their presence added chi energy to the group.

When their practice ended, they sat on the bench above the river. Birds were singing from nearby bushes.

"Today good for river cruise. I promise cormorant fishing. Staff bring us to river. Water good today, slow moving." Han had his arm behind Sally on the back of the bench. A breeze blew his uncombed hair. The morning sun shone through nearby trees and left a dappled pattern on his face.

Sally giggled, she couldn't help herself. He looked adorable. "You look like a boy today. I wish I had my camera. It's good to see you so super-relaxed." She reached for his hand and stood up. "A boat ride sounds great, but first I need to shower and change my clothes. Come on, let's go," and tugged his arm. They returned to their rooms to find the breakfast food had been cleared, and replaced with a vase of fresh flowers and bottled water. Sally heard a child's voice from inside her room. She opened the door to find a little girl playing with Li and his red ball on the floor. A young woman was cleaning the room.

She said to Sally, "She like cat."

"Would she like to stay with Li today while we go on a boat trip?" Sally asked.

"Mother say she can stay," Han translated. "Girl alone while mother work. Will be good with Li." He pulled her close and kissed her forehead. "We get ready for boat."

Dressed in a tee shirt and shorts, Sally stood outside her door waiting for Han. A picture of his tousled hair, dark eyes, muscular physique, and soft hands kept playing over and over in her head.

He came out of his room dressed in clean clothes and walked toward her with a strong confident stride. Sally thought, "He could be mine."

A WOMAN STOOD AT THE BOAT LANDING WITH FRESH flower garlands. She placed one on Sally's head, allowing the flowers and ribbons to encircle her hair. The boat was a two-seat narrow bamboo raft. Han sat behind her, so she could lean back against his chest. He put his arms around her and she held his hands for security. There weren't life preservers on the boat, and she didn't want to go swimming. The captain stood in the back and, with a long paddle, moved the boat out into the river.

The clear water flowed over river rocks. Green plants grew on the river bottom. A slight fish odor made Sally look down. She saw a long pole with a net at the end and realized the boat had done double duty as a fishing boat.

The captain wore a wide brimmed straw hat. He began to sing as he moved the boat slowly along the shoreline. Han leaned forward and sang softly in her ear. Sally began to loosen the fingers that clutched his arm.

As they moved up the river, she watched the hills, green and cone shaped. The tour book had said they each had a name. She wanted to find the nine horses painted in the hills by green trees.

They passed a man sitting on a log that extended into the river. He wore shorts and nothing else. His bare feet dangled in the water. He shook his head, and sent wet hair flying. Then dipped his shirt in the river and wrung it out. Sally realized he was bathing and washing his clothes.

After an hour, they came to a floating food bar. The captain helped them out and Sally and Han ate fish kabobs and drank bottled water.

Many of the boats turned to return, but they continued up stream. The captain unrolled a bamboo and cloth awning over their heads to shade them from the sun. At a turn in the river, Sally saw the cormorant fishing boats. They had formed a circle and the fishermen were yelling to attract the fish.

Sally watched the men tie a cloth around the birds' necks, then send them into the water with a command. Several birds disappeared under the water for three or four minutes. When they reappeared they had a fish in their bills. The fishermen took the fish and sent the birds out again.

Han told her, "Cormorants hold breath long time."

"They must be hungry. I feel sorry for the birds." Sally made a sad face.

Han pointed to a fisherman loosening his birds tie. "Bird eat small fish. Have job with man."

Sally leaned back against Han and closed her eyes. She was in a good place. She felt Han's kiss on her neck.

"This is a different experience from the cities I've visited. I'm glad you brought me here. I can relax without the city noise, and I'm breathing better. The rice fields and river are beautiful," her voice a bit plaintive. Sally remembered her time here was limited.

Han ran his hand along her arm. "There are more. I take you," he promised.

"I wish I had more time." Sally reached for his hand. "But I need to go back home. My home is in America. I have responsibilities there."

Han played with her blond curls. "I know. We have more days here. You say friends tell you to *let things happen.* We go water show tonight. Very beautiful."

On their return trip down river, the captain allowed his boat to float with the slow river current. Han sang with the captain. Sally, with her head back on his chest, an ear to his cotton shirt, listened to Han's heart-beat.

The staff car brought them back to the resort. In her room, Sally checked her supply of clean clothes. A long sleeve shirt and cargo pants for a cool night, a jacket she had found in Beijing. For later, after the show, there was nothing that even resembled a sexy nightgown. Her long tee shirt for sleeping had "Cape Cod" emblazoned on the front. Not a good time for a home reminder. She wondered if Han would be joining her. Did she need to ask him?

A BROCHURE FROM THE HOTEL LOBBY DESCRIBED THE Impression Sanjie Liu river show. Outdoor seats were cement and wood steps on a hillside. The Li River water basin was approximately two miles wide with twelve mountains in the background. It was believed to be the largest outdoor water arena in the world. The seventy-minute show was designed by the chief director of the 2008 Olympics opening night ceremony. It told China's history in seven episodes with a cast of 600 actors and actresses from local villages.

Their seats were in the middle of the hillside. Han bought a magazine from a man waving them in the air that explained the show in English.

The show opened with the sound of voices in the dark night. Hundreds of lanterns appeared on the river bank. Slowly the lights illuminated a village of people as they walked to the river. A story of China's history began in song. A fleet of small boats was gently pulled by poles through silent moonlight. Underwater platforms rose and sank to allow dancers on a tiny island in the middle of the river. Hundreds of soldiers walked across the river. The long haired women from Huangluo Village washed their hair. Farmers brought oxen onto platforms in the water. A baby fell in and was rescued. Always a cast of hundreds came to the river from left and right. The mountains were lit with colored spotlights. Sally was mesmerized. What an extravaganza!

Sally held Han's hand. Suddenly, she laughed.

"You laugh? When funny part? I not see," Han asked.

Sally whispered, "In America we have drive-in movies. When I was a teenager I sat in a car and watched a movie. I held hands with my boyfriend. Now I'm holding your hand. Like a teenager."

Han smiled and squeezed her hand.

CHANG BROUGHT THEM BACK TO THE HOTEL. HAN HELD

her hand as they walked to their rooms. "I stay with you tonight. Is that good?" He pulled her close and kissed her eyelids. A promise of more.

"I don't have a sexy nightgown."

Han let go of her. He opened his mouth to say something, then shook his head and laughed. A second try at speaking was unsuccessful.

"You are not being romantic," Sally had her hands on her hips.

"I always see beautiful woman," He pulled her close with a strength that made Sally shiver. Tight enough for her to feel him take a deep breath. "I don't have English words." He let her go, shook his head again. "I change clothes and come back."

The staff had left a bottle of wine and two glasses in her room.

Han returned in a clean white shirt and last night's shirt in his hand. He put his shirt on the foot of the bed for Li. The kitten immediately curled up on Daddy's shirt.

He opened the wine bottle and filled two glasses.

They sat together on the bed. She had been sitting close to Han all day and it had begun to feel natural. Her body responded to his touch.

Han was silent. He sipped his wine. Then, in a barely discernible voice, he said, "Have Chinese relationship question. Will you marry me?"

Sally's hand shook. "You almost got a wine bath."

She put the glass on the nightstand. Then her hand on his chest. He was trembling. "I can't say yes. You know that. But I want to be with you."

He nodded and kissed her. Their talking time was done.

HE WAS ASLEEP. SHE BROUGHT HER CELL PHONE AND Kindle into the bathroom. A text message to Aimee, the most modern of her Yangzhou girlfriends: "Han asked me to marry him. What do I do? I'm leaving in two days." An e-mail to Mary: "Han asked me to marry him. What do I do?"

A tiptoe return to her room, and she snuggled next to the man asleep in her bed.

SALLY WOKE WHEN SHE HEARD HAN LAUGH. HE WAS ON the floor, playing ball with Li. Seeing her eyes open, he came over and kissed her sleep face. "Sleep, I come back for breakfast."

She rolled over to his side of the bed and closed her eyes.

Li woke her. "*Meow*" announcing his food dish was empty.

After she performed her chef's services, she checked her cell phone and e-mail for messages. Mary's said: "Not without me!" Aimee wrote: "Get a ring!"

Han wore a Cheshire cat expression at the breakfast table.

Sally began to talk, "While you slept last night I sent messages to Mary and Aimee . . ."

"I not sleep, you not there."

She continued, "I asked them what I should do."

"I know, Frederick call."

"Aimee blabbed? Not good!"

"Blabbed?"

"Told Frederick."

With the same satisfied grin, he held a small carved wood box. "Chinese wife always tell husband."

"Not American woman." She couldn't say *"wife"*. "Aimee told me to get a ring."

"This ring?"

Sally looked at the box. Put her hand out to touch it, pulled back. She looked at Han, at the box. Then sat frozen.

He opened the box and took out a ring with a dark green rose encased in gold filigree. It had an old patina. "Mei help me buy jade ring. I tell her you want flowers. She find finger size when dress you for dinner date."

"When did you do all this?" She watched his hand with the ring move toward her.

"In Yangzhou, after you leave."

Han held the ring next to her left hand. His voice continued, soft, sincere, his hand shook, "You take?"

She raised her hand and he put the ring on her finger.

Nearby bushes exploded with cheers. Staff jumped out from their hiding places.

Sally looked at the grinning waiters and housekeeping women. "Does the whole world know about this?"

Han grinned and nodded. "Not world. School teachers in Yangzhou know. My students in Shanghai know. Mary in America know."

"You told Mary! When?"

"In Beijing, tell Mary I want you back in China. Tell I have ring. Ask you to be wife in China. She say you have husband. I say can have Chinese banquet, not go to registry office."

Sally looked at the jade rose ring. Michael had put a gold band on that finger twenty years ago. She had taken it off two years ago when she knew it was time for her to begin a new life.

She stood, told the staff *xiè xie,* and reached for Han's hand. "I need to practice Tai Chi. My nerves are jumping."

Han led her to the Tai Chi practice area near the bench overlooking the river.

THE LAST DAY IN GUILIN DISAPPEARED IN MOMENTS. SALLY showed her ring to all of the staff, then spent time on the phone with Mary, Aimee, and Mei. She played ball with Li and walked the garden paths with Han.

They took a morning plane shuttle to Shanghai. Sally's plane to Boston left that afternoon. She had made a reservation to spend the day at the airport private lounge.

Han held her backpack and Li in his bamboo box. She looked at him and said. "Please, I want to say good-bye now."

He nodded and slowly let go of the purple backpack. He held her head in his hands and whispered, "I wait for you, American girl."

CAPE COD

SALLY

Seagulls squawked their greeting. First one, then five, finally a flock of white and gray birds flapped their wings at Sally's bare feet. Each one called for a share of the breadcrumbs she tossed in the air. The tourists were gone. It was now the responsibility of the Cape Cod residents to supplement the spoiled birds' diet.

Sally loved October on the Cape. Skies were blue with puffy white clouds. The Atlantic Ocean waves changed from a quiet green to a ripple of blue, reached to the sky with a thrust, then bent with the weight of a white crest to fall, return, and begin again. She wiggled her toes in the wet sand. Salt water healed. She had come to allow nature to care for her.

Yesterday, she had gone to the hospital to visit Michael. His body no longer belonged to the man she married. Blond hair that once sparkled in the sun lay flat on his head, dull, lifeless. He could no longer smile at her, lure her to him with seductive blue eyes. He seemed so fragile under the protective sheet, as if her touch might break him.

She sat next to his bed and gently placed her right hand under his. It always surprised her that his flesh was warm. His hand was smooth. Calluses from his carpenter's hammer were gone.

"Michael, I have something to tell you." She began. Her lungs fought for breath. "I went to China. We never talked about going there. I went with Mary."

Sally leaned in. "China has an ancient history of beauty and brutality. I visited amazing temples built on the side of a cliff, knelt on silk cushions before Buddhas. They have city parks with flowers and trees and places to practice Tai Chi. Museums have porcelain figurines and rice paper paintings thousands of years old. They honor their past with holidays."

She touched the scar on his forehead. "Their cities have millions of people. The air is putrid. They hardly ever see the sunlight. The need for housing and industry has brought about building of skyscrapers everywhere. Thousands of tall buildings. They tear down *hutongs*, where people have lived for thousands of years, to build ugly condos. I remember you hated to destroy historic buildings to build new ones. I learned about wars in the past. There was so much I didn't know."

The jade ring on her left hand caught her breath. "I met all kinds of people. Chinese teachers, a British expat, travelers from France. I taught English to children." Another breath, "I met a man there. A good man. He wants me to be there with him." Breathing faster now, she needed to finish. "I've been offered a job there teaching English. For a year. I want to be with him, but I don't want to leave you."

As Sally wept, she felt a change. Her hand under his suddenly warmed. She felt it: the sensation of his love.

The alarm on his overhead heart monitor screeched and the line went flat.

She pushed the white button on her cell phone and heard it ring in China, twelve hours away. It was eight a.m., so it was night there. He would be home with their kitten.

"Hello, Sally," Han answered. "Li jump up and down when phone ring. He want to see you. I hold phone for him."

A Siamese kitten appeared on her screen and hollered, "*Meow!*"

"Hello, Li. I miss you too. But I want to talk to Daddy."

She studied Han's face, his brown eyes had dark circles beneath. His voice was hoarse. "I am here. I cook for us."

"I'm at the beach. I just fed the birds. I want to walk and hold the phone, so you can see and hear the waves. It will be like we're going for a walk together."

"I watch waves. Remember river boat ride."

Sally held the phone over her head and walked along the shoreline. She didn't know what to say. His pain was palpable across the miles.

She stopped and held the phone to her lips. "I remember everything. The children call to me, I see the flowers in the parks. I practice Tai Chi alone. I miss you, too. I'm coming back."

YANGZHOU FRIED RICE

Yangzhou fried rice is a white rice, or brown, made without soy sauce.
I use long grain white rice and cook in a small electric rice cooker.
That's how they do it in China. An electric rice cooker is amazing. Just
add rice, a bit of butter or oil, salt and water according to directions,
push the button and forget it. Always perfectly done. It can be he main
course, a side dish, a cold snack, and brought to pot luck dinners.

INGREDIENTS

3 Cups cooked rice

1 to 2 eggs

1 handful cooked shrimp chopped into small pieces

1 to 2 thick slices of deli ham chopped into small pieces

1 to 2 teaspoons sesame oil

Loosely scramble the eggs over medium high heat in a bit of vegetable
oil and remove from pan and break or chop into small pieces. Add
cooked rice to wok, Fluff, then ham and shrimp. Add 1 teaspoon
sesame oil and fluff again. Add onion to taste. You may want to add
the other teaspoon of sesame oil. Add scrambled egg with last fluffing.
You want to keep the egg light. This is a basic recipe and ham can be
eliminated for vegetarians, frozen peas and other chopped vegetables
can be added. Leftover chicken also works.

ACKNOWLEDGMENTS

I give thanks to the hundreds of authors who showed me the joy of reading. They taught me the magic of expressing myself with words on a sheet of paper.

Today I am grateful for the members of writer's groups on Cape Cod. The Memoir's Writers, Rising Tide Writers, Cape Cod Writer's Studio, and the Summer Fiction Writers Group. Each member has been irreplaceable with their support. They encouraged me, read my first drafts, continued to inspire and applauded when I declared I had a manuscript.

A special thank you to my Beta Readers. PJ Rainwater, who knew I was going to write this book before I did. Deb Cubillos, for finding comma's and apostrophe's, and Thom Huettner, for the all important male perspective.

A special thanks to my editor Virginia Aronson in Deerfield Beach, Florida.

ABOUT THE AUTHOR

I wrote my first stories, with a by-line, for The Central Crier high school newspaper in 1956. Then took a 60 year break.

In 2017 I wrote "The Life That Made Me, ME" a Memories for my family. A true story described a trip I took to China with three other women. I had so much fun writing and remembering that trip I decided I wanted to say more. "China Strong" is fiction based on dreams, memory and researched facts.

I am currently writing "Navajo Strong," a fiction.

96360427R00123

Made in the USA
Lexington, KY
21 August 2018